PRESCRIPTION
FOR ROMANCE

Ruth Mason came East to the small
New England hospital determined to forget her unhappy California love affair.

She thought she'd bury herself in her
work and think things out peacefully and
quietly.

Instead she was assigned to duty on
the night ward where she found love,
excitement and danger when she was
teamed with a society doctor . . . chased
by a psychopathic killer . . . and trailed
by a handsome young police officer.

SIGNET "Doctor and Nurse" Stories
You'll Enjoy

NIGHT
WARD

by

NOAH GORDON

A SIGNET BOOK

Published by THE NEW AMERICAN LIBRARY

To Sarah Melnikoff

© 1959 by Noah Gordon

All rights reserved

Tenth Printing

Signet Trademark Reg. U.S. Pat. Off. and Foreign Countries
Registered Trademark—Marca Registrada
Hecho en Chicago, U.S.A.

SIGNET BOOKS are published by
The New American Library, Inc.,
1301 Avenue of the Americas, New York, New York 10019

Chapter One

He was no more than seventeen. His face was burned from the wind and the sun, and his hair was straight and black. His teeth gleamed white when he grimaced in pain. He would have a nice smile, Ruth Mason decided.

"How is it, Tony?" she asked.

"It is no picnic, beautiful nurse," he said. It was what he had called her ever since he had come under her care that morning: "beautiful nurse." It was nice to hear, and she liked it. Pain makes time a relative thing. Tony had told her that afternoon that it seemed as if he had spent half his life on his back in this hospital bed. She was his friend, he said, and she had taken care of him for half a lifetime.

"Is there much pain?" she asked. "I can give you a needle if you want it. Something to put you to sleep."

"It feels as if it is still there," he said. They both looked down at the flat sheet where his right foot should have been. It had been amputated early that morning. "It feels as if the big toe is itching. If I could only scratch it, I think everything would be all right."

"Everything will be all right," she said. "Do you want the shot?"

"I am afraid to sleep," he said. "I think that I will dream of the big fish and how it happened. Do you have a needle that will keep me from dreaming?"

"No," she said, "but you probably won't dream, and the sleep will do you good."

"All right," he said. She came back in a few moments and gave him the hypodermic, and almost at once he felt the blessed numbness creeping through his body, spreading even to the big toe so that the itching went away.

"How is it, Tony?" Ruth Mason asked. Her voice sounded like a faraway chime.

"It is very good, beautiful nurse," he said.

The fishing boat was named Blessed Virgin. *In the cabin there was an embroidered picture of the Mother Mary, and whenever they remembered, each of the crew lit a taper and stuck it into the little tin candelabrum screwed onto the shelf in front of the picture. It was a very old boat but very fast, and it belonged to Tony's uncle, Rafe Rafiniello. Tony was first mate. Ever since his twelfth birthday he had gone out on the* Virgin *with Rafe and the crew of five, and for years he had been earning a man's pay by doing a man's work. Sometimes they seined and sometimes they fished with lines, depending on the bottom and the schools, but they usually brought back a loaded hold. It was a lucky ship and a lucky crew.*

That morning Rafe was in a good mood. "Hey, Tony, when you gonna buy half my boat, hey?" he had yelled as they cast off.

"When you bring the price down far enough," Tony yelled back. It was an old joke, but they were only half-joking. Rafe had no sons and Tony was saving his money.

A friendly Navy pilot had tipped Rafe off that tuna were making the water boil about six miles out, so he pointed the Virgin's *nose toward blue water and the blunt prow knifed through the Pacific, shuddering like a living thing when it crashed through a swell. Tony had worked hard on the way out, getting the barrels iced and salted down, and laying out the lines and the big hooks. When they reached the school it happened the way it sometimes did: one moment they were plowing through deep water and the next moment the* Virgin *was an island surrounded by a mass of silver-finned bonito.*

The whole crew lined the rail and started throwing out lines. No bait was used; when bonito are biting in school they strike at the empty hook, and, as fast as the crew could throw out lines, they hauled in flopping beauties. They had been taking fish for perhaps a quarter of an hour when the huge, dark shapes that were shovel-nosed

6

sharks began their slashing attacks on the tuna, ripping into the school with clicking jaws, rolling over on their backs as they attacked. Their white bellies made inviting targets. Rafe had a loaded rifle in the cabin, but his business was catching fish, not shooting sharks, and there was enough tuna for both sharks and fishermen.

Everything would have been all right if Tony hadn't broken one of the strictest rules on a fishing boat: Never let your line loop. There was a big loop in his line right on the deck. He stepped into it as a bonito grabbed the hook; before he could deck the tuna a huge shape split the water and took the bonito, hook and all. The shark turned on a dime and headed for sea, and, as the line whizzed out, the loop tightened around Tony's ankle with a sudden jerk that sent him crashing to the deck in pain. He felt himself being pulled into the sea, and he grabbed the deck rail and hung on. Then, as the pain washed over him, he kicked his leg in a vain, frantic attempt to free his ankle from the line. While he kicked, he screamed. And then he kicked some more.

Ruth was at the other end of the ward when she heard her patient screaming in his sleep. "He did dream, after all," she said under her breath. She was giving an old man his back-rub; as another tortured cry floated down the ward, she dried him hurriedly and replaced his pajama top.

"I'll drop in later to finish," she promised, then she walked swiftly down the corridor to Tony Rafiniello's room. He was still thrashing his leg wildly when she got there. He had banged the stump against the foot of the bed, and despite the heavy padding of bandage he must have reopened the artery. She saw with a sudden lurch of fear that blood was pouring through the bandage.

He was awake, his eyes wild with fear. Ruth knew that she didn't have time to call for a doctor: when an artery is open, the patient loses blood fast.

"Tony," she said. "You're awake now and everything is all right." As she spoke, her hands were busily ripping the bedsheet into strips. "I'm going to fix your leg again, Tony," she said, "but you mustn't kick any more. Do

7

you understand?" He nodded and lay back on his pillow, his head turned and his eyes closed.

It was the femoral artery, she knew. *The pressure point is in the thigh,* she told herself. She found it and looked around for something firm. There was a small pocket Bible on the table nearby, and she grabbed that and pressed it against Tony's leg. She tied the torn sheeting into a loop and used the crank from the hospital bed as a lever. It was an unprofessional-looking, makeshift tourniquet, but it was a tourniquet, and as she twisted it tighter and tighter it began to do its job. The pulsing gush of blood changed to a stream, then a trickle, and finally it stopped.

"I'm going to leave you for a minute, Tony," she said. "You'll be all right, but I want to get the doctor to fix you up."

"Okay, beautiful nurse," he said. His voice was thick and faint.

She knew that she had about fifteen minutes before the tourniquet would have to be loosened, but she also knew that he needed blood. She phoned the doctor and the blood bank, and in a few minutes the responsibility for Tony Rafiniello had been lifted from her shoulders.

"You did a good job," the doctor told her. "He couldn't have lost much more blood and lasted, but you stopped it fine. He should be all right in a couple of days."

She had only minutes to go on her shift, and she finished in a cloud of anticlimax and fatigue. In the nurses' lounge she stripped off her bloodstained uniform and rolled it into a ball. "If one of the other nurses wants to go to the trouble of cleaning this," Ruth told the attendant, "she can have a good uniform."

Her suitcase was all packed and waiting in her locker, and her trunk had been shipped that morning. She had said all the good-by's she wanted to say, but before leaving she obeyed an impulse to look in on Tony once more. He was awake; he gave her a tired grin when he saw her.

"Hello, beautiful nurse," he whispered. He cleared his throat. "They tell me you did me a good turn."

"I just wanted to say good-by," she said. She put out

her hand and he shook it, concern creeping into his eyes as he saw the suitcase.

"You will be back," he said.

She smiled. "No, Tony, I'm leaving California. I'm going East."

"But I need you," he said. "What will I do?"

"You'll do just fine," she said. "Best of luck."

"Luck," he said. She picked up her valise and left the room. Halfway down the corridor she heard his voice. "Beautiful nurse." She turned and went back. Tony was talking to the night nurse. "Beautiful nurse," he said, "could I have a little juice?"

She grinned wryly to herself as she got into the elevator. Patients like Tony were diplomats; he would, she thought, get along very well indeed. She walked through the town to the bus station. The 11:22 for San Francisco was all set to leave when she got there, and she climbed aboard and bought her ticket from the driver. She had just settled into her musty-smelling plush seat when the driver closed the door and the bus swung into life and rolled down the flat, wide main street. They were out of Monterey before she had time for one last look, and she leaned back and closed her eyes. She wanted to sleep, but she was a little afraid that she would dream about a big, dark shark. In a little while Salinas, too, had been left behind. The bus roared down Route 101.

Chapter Two

She hadn't realized how big a country it was. Flying across from San Francisco to New York, she'd been sorry that she hadn't taken a train and seen more. But now, sticky and full of self-pity in the ancient railroad car, she wished that she had flown from New York to Massachusetts. It was hot. Summer wouldn't hit New England officially for another nineteen days, but someone had neglected to brief the thermometer. It got hot in northern California, too, but the warmth there was a comfortable mixture of one part blazing sun and one part bay fogs and peninsula mists. This was a different kind of heat, full of juices that filled her pores and turned her clothes into sodden toweling. For four hours she had sat and watched the countryside roll by her window, a strange, alien land, hilly and rocky and light green from spring rain. It was pretty country, but there were stone walls instead of twisted rock-pines, and she felt like a stranger.

Two conductors had been sitting together in the last seat reading different sections of the Boston *Herald*. One of them was clean-shaven. The other, the one who wasn't, got up and walked down the swaying aisle without touching the seats. He gave her lithe blondeness a quick, approving glance as he passed by.

"DUT-TON!" he bawled, making it sound like two words. "Next station is Dut-ton. Change for connections to Boston and Providence."

Ruth felt her stomach muscles tighten as she watched the town take shape outside her window. It looked unappealing: outskirts of factories and scrap metal yards displaying rusted automobile corpses, and a layer of coal dust that covered everything. When she was a little girl her mother had described it to her as a place of white church steeples and red barns. Could the town have changed so much over the years?

There didn't seem to be a redcap, so she lugged her own valise; she could send for her trunk later. The terminal was a huge, vaulted mausoleum through which her footsteps echoed as she walked to the street. Every cab in town must have been lined up in front of the depot. The driver of the vehicle at the head of the long column jumped out and held the door for her, and she gratefully sank into the leather cushioning of the back seat.

"Fifty-one June Street," she said.

It was the address of the rooming house at which the hospital had arranged for her to stay, and the driver nodded and lurched the cab away from the curb. There was a folded newspaper on the seat beside her, and Ruth

10

picked it up. The Dutton *Morning Telegram*. She had become so accustomed to the appearance of the Monterey *Peninsula Herald* that this newspaper made her feel like someone pretending to be something she wasn't. Fighting against the thick loneliness rising in her throat, she started to read. The headline dealt with a crisis in the Middle East. She read the columns with little interest, but further down on the page a smaller story caught her eye:

IDENTITY OF KNIFE-MURDERER CONTINUES TO BAFFLE POLICE

Chief of Police William P. Corrigan announced last night the transfer of six officers to the Homicide Squad from various divisions of the Police Department.

"We are leaving no stone unturned," he said. "We will find the Johnson killer."

A reliable source last night revealed to this newspaper that Dutton police have uncovered no new leads in the May 12 slaying of Einar Johnson, 71. The homeless, unemployed house-painter was stabbed in the back four times, apparently while sleeping on a bench in Oak Park.

"It looks as if your police department is having its troubles," Ruth said. The cabbie didn't ask her what she meant. He knew.

"They ain't the only ones, lady," he said bitterly. "This is a scared town. Nobody's doing any business, this town is so scared. They're playing that story way down in the paper. We had four of these stabbings in the last two-three months, you know? This old guy in the park, though, he's the first one to be knocked off. You think a cabbie would do a thing like that?"

For a moment she couldn't follow the line of reasoning. "I don't know," she said. Then she caught a glimpse of his eyes glaring at her in the mirror. "No," she said hastily. "Well, of course not."

"You're very right," he said reproachfully. "But do people realize? No, all of a sudden every one of us drivers is a killer, just waiting to get a fare to a lonely road before pullin' the knife. The only ones ridin' the cabs come off the buses and trains, like you." He smacked a huge palm against the steering wheel. "Boy, if I could get my hands on that screwball."

"They'll get him," she said. "I spent a year working in a mental hospital in California. I saw a few of these cases. They get most of them in the end."

"Lady," he said, half-turning in his seat, "that's easy for you to say. You ain't a cab driver."

She fought with annoyance and lost. "No, I'm not," she said, "or I'd be watching the road." He gave himself the luxury of one last, disgusted look, then he hunched over the wheel in sullen silence.

As they left the manufacturing and business sections behind, she could see that it was a nice town. Shade trees, some of which must have dated back to the American Revolution, lined the residential streets. Twice they passed graceful, white church-spires pointing the way to the heaven of the Puritans. She tried to imagine her mother here as a young girl, but the past was so remote that even imagination couldn't bring her mother to life. Her father had been a Regular Army major, and all she remembered of him was the uniform and the raw smell of the pipe tobacco he had smoked. She had been fifteen when her parents had died in an automobile accident, but in eight years her memory of them had lost dimension. Now she had to struggle to remember their features, how their voices had sounded.

They were passing Memorial Hospital, a sprawling,

fence-enclosed collection of new-looking brick and granite buildings separated by wide expanses of green lawns. She was impressed, and she spoke spontaneously: "It's lovely. Do you know when it was built?"

The opening was made to order for her driver. "Lady," he said viciously, "this is a taxi, not a sight-seeing service. I don't come equipped with facts like that." The next three blocks were traveled in frigid silence; then the cab jerked to a halt in front of a large fieldstone and clapboard house. This time the hackie didn't bother to open her door.

"Eighty-five cents," he said, flipping the flag on his meter. Hating herself for her weakness, but glad to get rid of him, she tipped him and watched him drive his load of bitterness away with a clashing of gears. She carried her bag through the heat waves that bounced off the cement walk; then she rang the bell, standing in the glare of the sun and listening to the approaching footsteps. When the door opened and she stepped inside, the cool darkness of the hall hit her with a relief like pain. The woman who had opened the door was huge—fat, heavy-hipped, big-bosomed, and suffering from the humidity. Despite her evident discomfort, she smiled at Ruth as she mopped her neck with a wisp of silk handkerchief.

"Miss Mason?" she said. "I've been expecting you."

The bedroom was on the second floor. For a rooming house, the room was exceptionally comfortable and well furnished. The fat woman turned out to be Mrs. Hanscom, the landlady. "You'll like it here," she told Ruth confidently. "Everybody who lives here works at the hospital. I don't take outsiders, and the hospital keeps me filled up all the time. You want me to call you, or do you have an alarm?"

"I have an alarm," Ruth said. Mrs. Hanscom obviously wanted to talk, but Ruth was tired. She answered the landlady's bright comments politely, but shortly; looking disappointed, Mrs. Hanscom got the idea.

"Just call me if you need anything," she said.

Ruth promised. When she was alone, she lay back on the bed, listening to Mrs. Hanscom grunt her way down the stairs, and then listening to the silence. California was

13

far away. It was three o'clock in Dutton, but in Monterey people still hadn't had lunch. She closed her eyes against the heat of the room and thought what it would be like to walk once more straight into the surf and feel the wetness of the Pacific Ocean climbing her body.

After a while she got up and stripped down to her slip. The unpacking was easy, since her trunk hadn't arrived yet. She filled two drawers of the old chest, and in a couple of minutes nothing was left in the valise but a large photograph. She picked it up and stared at it. He was a confident, blond god, smiling at her out of the picture as if to say, "Don't be so tragic. Half the gags in Joe Miller's *Joke Book* are about girls who were left at the altar."

Probably if she could meet him face to face his actual words would be something very similar. As far back as she could remember, nothing had ever fazed Les Simons. He had an answer for everything. Everyone had always known that he was going to be a big man some day.

The trouble was, everyone had also known that he would marry Ruth—but he hadn't. She flopped back on the bed, holding the picture while she remembered how it had been when she had met him.

It had been in high school, with Les the Big Wheel—football captain and basketball star, as well as senior—and she an orphaned Army brat taken in by friends of her parents, who lived at Fort Ord. She closed her eyes and saw the gymnasium, decorated with too much crepe paper and a big sign stretched across the middle of the ceiling, reading !!! B*E*A*T S*A*L*I*N*A*S!!! It had been a pre-victory record hop, and she had been sitting in the gallery, alone and a little scared, watching the couples shuffling on the gym floor below. Suddenly he had been there in the seat next to her. For a long time they had just sat there and watched the dancers; then he had looked at her and smiled.

"Hi."

"Hi," she had said. Her voice had sounded queer and thin in her own ears, but somewhere she had found the courage to keep on talking. A few minutes later he had

asked her to dance and they had gone downstairs. They had danced every number together. Then, while a scratched record ground out "Good Night, Ladies," he had asked if he could take her home.

"I live way out at the Fort," she had said.

He'd grinned. "I've got a car." He had taken her home, and on the following evening they had gone to the movies. Before she knew what had happened, she was "Les's girl."

It had made a lot of difference. Going out, meeting friends, becoming conscious that she was a beautiful female, had changed her whole life. She had become alive. They had done the usual things teen-agers do in California, baking their bodies bronze in the sun, diving for abalones, dancing to portable-radio music on the hard-packed white sand, posing dramatically on surfboards whenever they had the equilibrium to pose. It had been light-hearted and fun until one night at a beach party. She and Les had found themselves apart from the crowd. They had been quiet, but suddenly he had spoken hesitantly.

"I think I love you, Ruthie."

For a moment it had frightened her into panic, but then she had looked at him, smiling and tousle-haired, standing in front of her with the light of the fire dancing on his blond head.

"You're like a little boy," she had said, and her hand had taken his and held it fiercely for a moment. After that for Ruth there had been no question of lots of dates with lots of boys. Les Simons and Ruth Mason were going to get married some day when they were older, and everyone knew it.

When she had been graduated from high school, Les was already at Stanford, playing "much football," as one sports-writer put it, and majoring in mechanical engineering. Ruth had a good scholastic record. Her marks had been high enough to have won her a scholarship, and she had some insurance money for her education. She had considered going to Stanford, but after lengthy discussion they both had agreed that nursing was a much sounder idea, since it would take only three years instead of four.

15

"The big dough will be going to engineering guys with graduate degrees," Les had explained. "This way, you can keep us going as a nurse while I go to grad school." It had sounded like a good idea, and when she had entered training she had discovered that, for her, nursing fulfilled a need to be of service. No duty had been too onerous, no drudgery too boring, and each new day had been better than the last. She had found a miracle in the processes of a healing human body. She had been capped on the same day Les had received his degree. They would have been married then, but he faced military service.

"Let the Navy have me first," he had grinned. It had seemed the practical thing to do, but before he left to report to Mare Island he had given her an engagement ring.

It had turned out to be a long engagement.

For two years he had had sea duty, and she had seen him only on rare, longed-for occasions. Then he had been assigned to San Diego, and she had expected to see him more often. But it was a long trip across the face of California. His visits had become less and less frequent, and so had his letters.

"Shore life agrees with me," he had written in one note. "Lots of wine and song." He could have given her the whole quotation. They had mutual friends who enjoyed going out of the way to report having seen him with other women. Ruth had hoped that once he was discharged she would find the boy she had known in the stranger he had become. She used to conduct a constant debate within herself. He's just kicking up his heels, the way every man does when he's in the service, *one voice would say.* Service doesn't spoil a man, *the other voice would reply fiercely,* it just emphasizes his real traits. *It might have developed into quite an oratorical contest, but Les himself had ended it by marrying the very available daughter of a very wealthy San Diego shipbuilder. A member of Ruth's bridge club had informed her one night that the girl was lovely, and that Les was going back to school for a master's degree in marine engineering.

16

For as long as she could, Ruth had taken the sympathy, the sudden switches in conversation when she joined a group, the deadly gaiety of the parties thrown by her friends to fill her empty evenings. Then one morning, after having spent a sleepless night tossing and asking herself where she had failed him, she had decided to go away. At first she had thought of enlisting, but the idea of using the Nurse Corps as a refuge from her personal problems was both distasteful and melodramatic. Then she had remembered her mother's stories about the New England town in which she had grown up. Ruth had no relatives in Dutton, but there was nothing holding her in California. She had written to the superintendent of nurses at Memorial Hospital and had received an immediate job offer. On her last morning in California she had walked alone down the wind-swept beach, saying good-by to a lot of young memories.

Now, tired and scared and more unsure of herself than she had been in years, she lay on the lumpy mattress of a boardinghouse bed in Massachusetts and fought back the tears. There was an inscription on the photograph. *To my Ruthie. With all my love. Your Les.* It had been only last-minute weakness which had made her take the picture with her at all, and now the sight of the smiling male face and the arrogant blackness of the handwriting infuriated her. It reminded her of her failure to succeed in the thing she had wanted most. In sudden fury she gripped the photograph and pulled at it; there was a thick cardboard frame, but finally it ripped in two and she tore the pieces automatically until they littered the bed. Then, sobbing like a scared child, she buried her face in the mattress and tried not to think.

Mrs. Hanscom, carefully holding a beaded pitcher that tinkled, came up the stairs a few minutes later. At Ruth's door she paused and knocked.

"How about a glass of lemonade?" she called. There was a brief silence. When Ruth finally refused, her voice was collected, but the older woman had caught the undertone of hoarseness, and she had dealt with boarders for a long time.

17

"All right, dearie," she called. Shaking her head, she waddled down the stairs again. She eased herself into a chair near the television set, which was tuned to a baseball game. The Red Sox were at bat, and as Ted Williams stepped to the plate Mrs. Hanscom poured herself a large glass of lemonade and drained it thirstily. Then, as Williams flied out to center field, she got up, sighed, and switched channels until she found a soap opera that would make her cry, too.

Chapter Three

It was nine o'clock when Ruth awoke. At first she didn't know where she was, and she lay in the darkness of the strange room waiting for the nightmare to pass. But then she remembered, and she pulled herself off the bed and snapped on the light. The scraps of torn photograph still littered the room, and she gathered them up and put them in the wastebasket.

"So long, Buster," she said aloud.

The shower was at the end of the hall, but it was good and she stayed in it a long time, letting hot needles thrum themselves against her body, and finishing off with a burst of cold that made her see green ice when she closed her eyes. She toweled hard, and by the time she got back into her room she was no longer ready to die. Her uniforms had been packed carefully, and she had to use her traveling iron only on the creases where they had been folded. She put on her newest one, and then, garbed in white protective armor, she left the house.

With the sun gone, the evening heat was soft and pleasant. She took her time strolling to the hospital, seeing all she could of the neighborhood in the early evening darkness. It was after ten when she knocked on the door lettered ALICE BOND, SUPERINTENDENT OF NURSES.

Miss Bond proved to be an efficient-looking woman with steady eyes and iron-gray hair. As soon as the amenities had been concluded, she opened a manila folder before her on the desk.

"You've had good training," she said. Her finger traced down the typewritten page of Ruth's application; then it stopped at an item. "What made you take the postgraduate course in obstetrics at San Francisco General?"

"I like obstetrical nursing. We've made birth safer, but we can't abolish labor pains. I feel that mothers should be in highly trained hands."

The superintendent nodded. "Of course," she said. "Do you think it will make you unhappy to do ward work, since at present there is no shortage of obstetrical nurses at this hospital?"

"I'm very happy working in the wards."

"I'm curious, Mason," Miss Bond said, "as to why you chose us, instead of one of the institutions closer to your home. How did you hear about us?"

All it requires, Ruth told herself desperately, *is a stock reply;* but she could feel her face flush and she was all out of stock replies. "I'd been told that years ago this was a nice town," she said.

Miss Bond stared, then she laughed. "It's a city now, Mason," she said dryly. "With almost a quarter of a million people in it. If you have any doubts, wait until it seems that most of them are assigned to your ward. We have five hospitals in Dutton. All of them are severely understaffed." She lifted her pen from its holder and held it poised above Ruth's card.

"The ideal arrangement would be to start you in gradually, but we can't do that. Any R.N. with your experience must be given charge of a ward. You'll take Revere, which is a big one. But actually it shouldn't be too hard for you to adjust: sick people act the same way all over the country. Can you work nights? That's when we really need you."

"I have no other obligations," Ruth said.

The older woman's eyes were understanding. "You're on from eleven to seven, then," she said. Her eyes took in the uniform. "You look ready to go to work. But you've been traveling today. If you're too tired to begin tonight. . . ."

Ruth rose. "Thank you," she said, "I had a long sleep." Miss Bond's handshake was quick and warm, an efficient but hearty dismissal. Ruth could feel the superintendent's eyes on her back as she walked out of the office.

The elevator operator let her off at the third floor. "Revere is on the east side of the building," he said, "straight down the corridor." She walked through the dark hollowness of the long hallway, listening to the familiar sounds: from one room a lonely whimper; from another a shrill, animal-like scream of pain; from a third the short, hacking cough which meant a lung had collapsed and the bellows that is the human chest was working overtime.

There was nobody in the nurses' station when she reached the ward, but a few minutes later a nurse came hurrying in, and Ruth saw by the keys dangling from her pocket that she was in charge.

"I'm your relief," Ruth said. "Ruth Mason."

The girl looked grateful. "Ann O'Leary," she said. "You're twenty minutes early, but am I glad to see you! Things are quiet now, but for a while I thought the roof was caving in."

"I can remember shifts like that."

The book she signed was slightly different from the one she had signed daily in California, but it meant the same thing: *With this signature I take on my own conscience the terrible responsibility for these sick and injured human beings.* She accepted the drug-closet keys and pinned them on her own belt.

"Watch out for Lambert in 318," the other girl was saying. "She's getting intravenous feedings and she walks in her sleep. Last week she went the whole length of the corridor with the needle still in her arm and the bottle dragging. We've got her strapped, but she needs checking." Ruth nodded. One of the first things she would do was scan the charts and familiarize herself with her patients.

"You'll find they keep you hopping," the other nurse said, after completing her report. "Besides yourself you have only one other R.N. I'll wait and introduce you."

Ruth could see she was eager to be off, and she smiled. "You go ahead," she said. "I'll introduce myself." With a tired wave, O'Leary disappeared down the corridor, grateful for the chance to get away. Ruth sat down at the chrome-topped desk and took the first of the charts off the rack. *Zamboski, Greta. Age, 51.* She read with mechanical interest the detailed report of the disease which was eating away the liver that had enriched Greta Zamboski's blood for over half a century. A green light on the panel board began flickering on and off before she had finished a page, and she hurried down the corridor toward Room 318, led more by the call than by the flickering light above the door. It was the same call she had answered so many times before. One word, this time as always, full of pain and impatient pleading.

"Nurse."

She played her flashlight into 318 and then snapped on the room light. Lambert, she saw with something of a shock, couldn't have been more than twelve years old. One year younger, she told herself automatically, and the girl would have been in the children's ward. But now she was Ruth's problem, and she dealt with it. A sleepwalker, O'Leary had said. Evidently she had tried to walk in her sleep this time, too, but the strap had held and the intravenous-feeding bottle had caught in its holder, ripping the needle from the girl's flesh and waking her. Now she sat up in bed and shook as she cried, a homely little girl in a grownup world of pain, her straight hair straggling lank and limp over her contorted face. Ruth shot a swift glance at the nameplate at the foot of the bed. First name, Evelyn.

"There, Evvie, it's all right. I'm here." She stanched the blood with an alcohol pad, deftly reinserted the needle and started the flow of glucose. Then she bathed the girl's face. It was a small face, full of the fears of a trapped creature. Evelyn Lambert was trembling. Her eyes sought Ruth's.

"You go back to sleep now," Ruth said.

The girl spoke for the first time. "Hold me." It was a plea rather than a demand.

Ruth knelt by her bed for a moment and put an arm

21

around the thin shoulders. "You go to sleep," she said, "and in the morning I'll give you the best alcohol rub you've ever had in your life. Is it a deal?" She adjusted the flow of the glucose and hurried back to the station.

The other nurse was there, preparing a hypodermic. She was a freckle-faced brunette named Peg Collins. They were introducing themselves when two lights began to flash on the board and a voice from a third room called for a nurse. They went in different directions. Ruth walked swiftly down the darkened corridor. Monterey still seemed half a world away, but suddenly she didn't feel very far from home.

The nights passed, one by one. Hospitals are places where friendships are easily made, and before her first week was through she was on terms of easy familiarity with the people with whom she worked. Revere Ward, in the form of a letter U, took up the third floor of an entire hospital wing. The left arm of the U was the men's section of the ward and the right arm was the women's section with the nurses' station and treatment rooms joining the two. Sixteen beds in each section, never empty for more than a few hours. Thirty-two patients, all needing careful nursing. At night many of them slept or were under sedation, but the ones who were left made a big job for two nurses. The hospital kept several nurses on duty at night as "floaters," to fill in wherever they were needed; but, being new and unproved, Ruth didn't want to call for help unless she absolutely needed it. Luckily, Collins was a good nurse who wasn't afraid of work.

There were times when the two of them raced frantically to restore order to a ward suddenly turned into a place of chaos. And there were other times when silence settled over Revere like a blanket. When this happened, Collins would sink gratefully into a chair and massage her aching ankles. Ruth hated the silence and the darkness, the invitation to set her mind thinking thoughts that led only to unhappiness. Instead, she busied herself with extra duties and made Collins slack-jawed at her efficiency. But moments came when there was simply nothing to be

22

done, and when this happened she tried to fill the void with conversation.

On her third night at Memorial a lull occurred at 3:00 A.M. Ruth worked for a while on some reports, and then she sat facing the dark panel of room signals, smiling at Collins, who was yawning.

"What made you become a nurse?" she asked. She had meant it as a sardonic joke that took in the unnaturalness of their working hours and the other's sore feet. But Collins took her seriously. She thought for a while.

"I think it was probably because of a cat I once had that died," she said.

It was a question Ruth had heard asked and answered a great many times, but this was a switch.

"What do you mean?" she asked.

"When I was a kid we lived on a farm in Brookfield," Collins said. "My father was a dairy farmer. It was hard work, making a living on a Massachusetts farm in those days, but we had a pretty good time. There were four of us kids: my sister Rita, my sister Mary, my brother Mikey, and me. We each had an animal all our own. You know, sort of a special pet?" Ruth nodded. "Well, mine was a big old cat called Tabby. Tab for short. It was a bad name for this cat, because he was a tom, but at the time I didn't know the difference. He was just about the biggest cat I ever saw, a black and white baby tiger, almost."

"And this cat told you to go out into the world and become a nurse?" Ruth smiled.

Collins didn't smile back. "No. But, you see, one day my brother Mikey killed the cat. We were in the barn, and it was hot and stuffy. It was one of those crazy days that all kids have. It was raining outside; that's how we happened to be playing in there—ordinarily my father wouldn't allow it. We used to act kind of wild, you know how kids do, throwing things at each other and all that. Well, Mike sneaked away and climbed up in the loft. There was this big sack full of feed near the edge of the haymow, and Mike just pushed it over the edge. It hit the cat, and the cat died as soon as we rolled the sack off him."

23

The two girls looked at each other in silence. They could hear the ticking of the clock in the hall.

"I really loved that cat," Collins said. "A little while later one of my father's cows got sick and he called the vet. The vet cured the cow. I know now that nothing would have saved my cat, but I thought then that if I had called the vet he would have made Tab well. I started asking for books about vets at the school library. They didn't have many, but they had lots of books about doctors and nurses. I started reading them, and I guess I've never stopped."

"What about Mikey?" Ruth asked.

"Mike? He's got a used-car lot in Lynn. He probably doesn't even remember I ever had a cat. I haven't thought of Tab myself in years." They looked at each other and they both started to laugh. "How about you?" Collins asked. "What made you become a nurse?"

A man once told me it would be a good way to help him toward a graduate degree, Ruth thought. "I figured it was the best opportunity to get to marry a rich, handsome young doctor," she said. "By the time I found out how wrong I was, I was enjoying nursing too much to stop."

"I know of only one doctor in the whole world who's young, handsome *and* rich," Collins said. "He's a resident right here at Memorial. Name of Alden MacKenzie. But as far as young MacKenzie is concerned, nurses are robots created to follow him, wheeling the dressing-cart."

"I've met those," Ruth said. "Grim, resolute men of science, with no time for frivolities like women. Secretly he probably wants to grow a long beard but doesn't dare."

But Collins was shaking her head. "No," she said. "That's the funny thing about him. Oh, he's *good* all right. I've heard other doctors say he's got a real talent for pathology. And he's no stuffed shirt. But every girl in the hospital has been trying to date him, and he acts as if we're fraternity brothers or something. Dr. MacKenzie just doesn't date nurses."

Ruth's interest was aroused. "Why?" she asked. Is he

24

one of those rank-conscious snobs you meet every once in a while?"

"He's no snob," Collins said quickly. "But everyone thinks that the real reason he has to be careful about dating is his mother."

"His *mother!*" Ruth said. "That makes him sound like a little boy."

Collins opened her mouth to explain, but before she could the lights on the panel began to flash again. "I'll get the next installment tomorrow," Ruth said. But the following night turned out to be a busy eight hours, and she forgot all about the dating habits of Dr. MacKenzie.

Chapter Four

Perry Watts was a quiet, meek man who led a quiet, meek life. Except for a passion for pinochle, and a secret desire to be an adventurer, which manifested itself in his reading every science-fiction magazine on the newsstands, Perry Watts was a perfect example of a home-trained, milk-fed American husband saddled with an overbearing, nagging wife. He was at peace during the day when he tended his business, which was Dutton's most cluttered hardware store; at night he became a second-class citizen. Someone once described Cynthia Watts as a dragon with phonograph needles instead of teeth. She never stopped talking, and whenever she talked she nagged Perry. Actually they loved each other deeply, but the casual observer would never have been able to guess this.

"I'd better get along to the garage and pick up the car," he said. He had had to leave the Chevvy for a battery charge, and now, as he attempted to leave the house and go to call for it, he experienced his usual difficulties in escaping his wife's presence.

"Why couldn't Jake Rourke over at the garage have

done it in the afternoon?" Cynthia asked for the fourth time.

The real reason was that there was a pinochle game scheduled at Jake's garage, and despite all the risks attached to his getting away from Cynthia, Perry hungered and thirsted for a good session of pinochle. He reached over and pecked Cynthia dutifully on one ruddy cheek.

"You know mechanics, dear," he said. "You can't rush 'em. Try, and they do a patchy job, just out of spite." He put on the sweater Cynthia's sister had knit for him two Christmases before. It was snug, and since he was small and skinny and wore glasses it gave him the appearance of an aging Mr. Peepers, but he put it on whenever he went out into the night air. "I don't think I need my umbrella, do you, Cyn?"

Cynthia didn't answer, so he waved vaguely in her general direction and stepped through the kitchen door and out into his back yard. The Watts home was a small, fairly new house in a large, fairly new development. It hadn't come with a back yard fence, and Perry had never bothered to put one up. Neither had his neighbors—all younger couples with small children—since their offspring ran from yard to yard all day long. Cynthia pretended that they were a bother, but Perry knew that it was a sorrow to her that their own union had never been blessed with a child, and he noticed that she always kept a cooky jar full for small visitors.

Only the Fossners at the far end of the development had bothered to put up a fence, an action which had made them the pariahs of the neighborhood. Now, as Perry crossed through the back yards to save time in his beeline to Jake's and pinochle, he mumbled in annoyance when he came to the Fossners' fence.

"Blast!" he said to himself. It was a satisfying expletive he had picked up in his science fiction reading—breaking none of the rules set up by his church, of which he was an elder, and yet giving all the satisfaction of a juicy swear-word. The fence was made of low pickets; faced with the alternatives of either crossing it or making a time-wasting detour, Perry climbed over somewhat stiffly, holding his breath and hoping that none of the neighbors was watching. In the street beyond the Fossner bungalow he quickened his pace, then found to his disgust that the lace of his right shoe had come untied. At first he tried to finesse it, keeping the shoe on by arching his foot and limping slightly, but halfway down the block he gave up in disgust and kneeled to tie his shoelace.

The man must have been standing in the shadows of a big elm only a few feet away. Perry didn't hear him until he felt the sharp pain of the blade entering his back. Then he heard a muffled little grunt, of either satisfaction or exertion. He had never been stabbed before, but he had been reading the stories of the "mad knifer" in the newspaper, and he knew what it was immediately. He dropped onto his face, fear and regret washing over him in a sudden wave as he fought to scream but could not. Unconsciousness, he thought wildly, was a little like a space voyage. There was a sensation of falling, and then vast, impenetrable darkness closed in over Perry Watts.

It had been a bad night. Surgery had been busy that morning and there were four post-operatives, each sufficiently recovered from anesthesia to be cranky and demanding. Ruth had arrived at Revere Ward just as a critical coronary case came in needing oxygen. The only oxygen tent in the ward was over a man with pneumonia-congested lungs, but in the emergency she had to take his unit and send a rush call for another. There was another serious heart case that had come in that afternoon, but the woman had hired a special nurse, and so Ruth and Collins didn't have to worry about her.

It was after one-thirty when they brought Perry Watts into Revere Ward. At midnight Ruth had heard a rumor —from the night elevator operator—that another knifing victim had been found and taken to the hospital. At the time of this report, Perry Watts was lying on his stomach in the basement operating room, while the skilled, blunt fingers of Dr. John Gottlieb, the hospital's chief surgeon, sewed together part of his trapezius muscle.

Ruth heard Cynthia Watts's voice first as the elevator at the end of the hall opened and Perry Watts was wheeled into Revere, surrounded by his entourage. Dr. Gottlieb was still in surgical whites, his mask pulled down and hanging by its cord from his neck. The joining of severed muscles is a delicate, tricky business, and the strain still showed on his face, but there was anger there, too. The moment Ruth heard what Mrs. Watts was saying, she understood why.

"We should have called in a specialist," she said. "Some man from Boston."

"Madam," Dr. Gottlieb said, "that was your privilege, and no one tried to persuade you to do otherwise."

"Well, they told me you were a good doctor," Cynthia said, "but now you say you don't even know if Perry's going to have full use of his left arm. Nobody told me anything like that before."

Dr. Gottlieb heaved a resigned sigh. "Look," he said, "your husband was brought in here critically injured. He lost a lot of blood. He's lucky that he didn't bleed to death, like that poor old man in the park, before they found him. We did the best we could for him, and he has a very good chance to get well." He turned his back on Cynthia Watts and spoke to Ruth. "Put him on whole blood, 3500 cc. before morning. And no visitors." Here he shot a glare at Cynthia. "Absolutely no visitors. Call Dr. MacKenzie if you have any questions." He strode away, his white gown blending into the dark corridor until he looked like a retreating ghost.

Ruth wheeled Perry Watts into 331, which was empty; then she helped the attendants transfer the unconscious man from stretcher to bed. They were skilled and gentle, but it was fortunate that Perry was still anesthetized. He groaned with pain even in his unconsciousness, and, when finally he lay face down on the bed, Ruth felt as if she had been through an ordeal herself. Hurrying out to phone for the blood, she ran into Cynthia Watts. Having watched her crusty performance with Dr. Gottlieb only a few minutes before, Ruth was astounded by the change which had come over the woman. She stood like an over-grown lost child, her forehead pressed against the wall and her face wet with tears.

"Will you take care of him?" she asked.

"Go home, Mrs. Watts," Ruth said softly. "We'll take care of him."

"Can't I sit in a chair in the hall?" the woman begged. "I won't bother anyone." It was easy to see that she was sincere, but Ruth thought of a busy night complicated by Cynthia Watts's presence in the hallway, and she suppressed a shudder.

"You go home, dear," she said. "He's in the best place he can be, under the circumstances. Dr. Gottlieb is a fine doctor. In the morning I'm sure you'll find your husband improved. Perhaps you can talk with him then."

She smiled wistfully as she watched Cynthia walk away. At first glance the little man in 331 and the overbearing woman who was his wife seemed to have little in common, but whatever they had was evidently something very fine.

The first 500 cc. of blood arrived from the blood bank, and she had just finished administering it when Revere Ward had two more visitors. The first, Ruth recognized as the uniformed city policeman assigned to regular duty in the hospital parking lot.

"I'm Gallagher, Ma'am," he told Ruth. "I guess you'll have me in the way for a while. They want a police guard here twenty-four hours a day, in case the guy who cut him wants to have another try at it." He motioned toward his plain-clothes companion. "This young bucko is Detective-Sergeant Ed Gillis of the Massachusetts State Police."

Gillis put out his hand. The state policeman was in his early thirties. One word flashed through Ruth's mind as she shook his hand: *tough.* He had an appealing but homely face. Somehow he reminded her of a Lincoln with a shorter, bashed-in nose. His eyes were brown and steady. When he spoke his voice was soft, but crisp and decisive.

"I'm going to keep Gallagher company," he said. "As soon as your patient comes to, I want to question him to see if I can get a lead."

"Sorry," Ruth said, "you won't be able to see him."

Gillis had taken his jacket off and was in the process

29

of loosening his tie. Now he paused and looked at her blankly.

"Pardon?"

"Doctor's orders are that Mr. Watts gets no visitors until at least tomorrow morning," she said. "I'm afraid you won't be able to see him."

"Is it critical?"

Ruth got out Perry Watts's chart. "He hasn't been placed on the critical list. There seem to be no signs of internal bleeding. But it's impossible to tell in cases like this one. That's why the doctor wants to wait. The patient is getting transfusions to make up for the blood he lost, and if there are no complications you can probably question him sometime tomorrow."

"And if there are complications?" The brown eyes bored into her, and Ruth felt herself flush with anger.

"If there are complications, Sergeant, anything can happen." She started to turn away, but he stopped her with a hand on her arm.

"Look," he said. His voice was soft, almost gentle. "You know what a policeman's job is?" There was a light flashing above the doorway of 318. Evelyn Lambert had probably had another nightmare.

"Only vaguely, Sergeant Gillis. I'm sure I'd love the complete course, but right now one of my patients seems to need me." She turned to go, but the hand, the big, square, cop's hand, was still on her arm and he didn't let go.

"This is a big state, nurse," he said in the same flat voice. "In this city alone there are 250,000 people, all afraid to walk down a dark street for fear what happened to Perry Watts tonight will happen to them. And do you know something?"

She was controlling a strong urge to knock his hand from her arm. "What?" she asked.

"They're right. This maniac or whatever he is can kill as many people as he wants to, because we don't have any idea what he looks like. So I'll just wait until Perry Watts comes around and then I'll ask him a few questions." He dropped her arm and threw himself into a chair near the grinning Gallagher.

Ruth headed for room 318, but on the way she stopped at the nurses' station. "Get Dr. MacKenzie up here right away," she said crisply.

By the time she had quieted down Evelyn and returned to the station, MacKenzie had arrived. He was big and blond, dressed in whites, but with his hair still tousled from sleep. Seeing him, for a moment her stomach gave a sudden lurch; she almost called out Les Simons' name. But then he turned toward her, and she realized that, full face, there was no resemblance at all. This face lacked the easy arrogance. Dr. Alden MacKenzie fitted Collins' description of him in that he was young and attractive, but there were shadows of self-doubt in his eyes, and Ruth liked the gentle humor-lines that creased the corners of his mouth when he smiled.

"I hear you're having trouble with the gendarmes," he said. "What's the story?"

Briefly, she relayed Dr. Gottlieb's orders and explained that the detective insisted on questioning Perry Watts. The resident nodded gravely. He strolled over to the policemen and sat down beside them, pulling out a pack of cigarettes. Soon MacKenzie and Gillis were engaged in a quiet, but heated, conversation. It went on for some minutes, until finally Gillis jammed his cigarette savagely into an ash tray, flung his coat over one shoulder and strode away in the direction of the elevator.

MacKenzie came back, unsuccessfully smothering a yawn which revealed strong white teeth. "Anything else bothering you girls, like sick people, for example?" he grinned. "If not . . ." They nodded, and he headed back for the softness of his bed.

"Well?" Collins said to Ruth. "Was I right about Mac?"

"You said he was young, handsome, and rich," Ruth said. "I don't know how much money he has." They relaxed for the first time in hours as they laughed, feeling the release from tension slide over their bodies like a warm bath.

But their good humor didn't have long to live. It died at 4:25 with Greta Zamboski in room 304. She had been a Catholic, and Ruth had just time to summon a priest for the last rites of her church before the end

31

came. Death is part of a nurse's job, but it is a hated part. Ruth had never been able to accept lightly the spectacle of the cessation of a human life, and at seven o'clock she left Revere Ward with the bitter taste of mortality in her mouth. On her way out, she stopped in to look at Perry Watts. He was conscious, but pale.

"How are you this morning?" she asked. He swallowed. When his voice came out of his throat it was a weak whisper.

"Do they have science fiction in the hospital library?"

She generally stopped at Mercier's Diner for coffee on the way home, preferring to eat her two big meals at lunch and dinner. This morning the place was crowded, but there was a seat left and she slid into it, reaching for the menu out of habit.

"Well," a voice said next to her, "were there complications?" On her right was Detective-Sergeant Ed Gillis, chewing on the end of a French cruller. There had been no belligerence in his tone, and Ruth decided to go along with his mood.

"No complications, apparently," she said. "If the doctor says it's okay, you can probably question him this afternoon."

"May I buy you a cup of coffee?"

She hesitated and he grinned. He didn't look at all tough when he grinned.

"As a peace offering?" she said.

"As a peace offering."

"I take mine black."

She studied him over the rim of the thick coffee mug. His eyes were bloodshot, and there was a purple stubble of beard on his chin and cheeks.

"You look as if you've been up all night yourself," she said.

"I drove all the way up from Holden Barracks when I heard about the stabbing," he said. "I haven't even had a chance to arrange for a place to stay with the local barracks yet. I've been drinking coffee in here for hours, trying to figure this case out." He reddened. "I'm sorry I pushed too hard last night. I've only been off a motorcycle for three weeks. I'm a detective on a temporary appointment, and if I want to stay in plain clothes I have to make good."

"From what I read in the papers, you've got yourself a tough nut to crack," Ruth smiled.

"They're all tough, but somehow they can all be cracked," Gillis said. "I don't expect to do it overnight. I'll be around town for a while." He looked at her ringless fingers. "You married?"

"No. Are you?"

"No. Perfect arrangement. Why don't we take in a movie or go bowling some night before you go on duty?"

For a moment she wanted to so badly that she trembled; a little of her coffee sloshed over the rim of the cup and dripped into the saucer. But then something within her felt very frightened.

"I can't," she said.

"Oh?" Gillis grinned a crooked grin. "Boy friend? I have a record for reaching pretty girls just after they've been claimed."

"Nothing like that," she said. "I just can't. Thank you for the coffee. I hope you solve your case, Sergeant." She slid off the stool and walked out the door. Gillis watched her through the glass windows of the diner until she was out of sight.

A waiter had been carefully monitoring the conversation, and now he chuckled as he wiped the counter. "Tough, Sarge," he said. "Some girls just don't appreciate a good opportunity when it comes along. You'd think you were asking her for a loan instead of a date."

Gillis leaned forward. "I have a favor I'd like to ask you," he said gently.

The man gawked. "What is it?" he asked.

Gillis fixed him with an icy stare. "How about bringing me another French cruller?"

That night when Ruth relieved Ann O'Leary, she asked very casually if there were any new developments in the Perry Watts case.

"He seems to be doing well," O'Leary said. "They've still got a policeman guarding him around the clock, and a reporter from the *Telegram* was here to interview him. His wife keeps phoning to find out his condition. I give her two more days before she starts lugging in chicken broth from home. I know the type."

"There was a state police detective here last night," Ruth said. "Has he been back?"

"Oh, yeah. A big guy. Looks like a gentle gorilla. He was here for a long time this afternoon. I heard him say he'd be back with a stenographer."

It was a long, quiet night, whose greatest challenge was that she had to awaken Evelyn Lambert twice for streptomycin injections. The child had a Proteus infection. Ruth had met Proteus cases before, and she knew that the microbe is one of the most difficult to kill. It carries its own "armor plating" that completely surrounds it, and only one or two drugs are capable of piercing this germ armor. Streptomycin is one of them. Waking the girl always brought on a brief nightmare until she realized what was going on. Ruth hated inserting the needle into the already bruised and pierced flesh, but the doctor had left written orders. She knew that if the infection progressed far enough, the kidneys would deteriorate.

She found that by rubbing the back of the girl's neck and whispering her name, she could awaken Evelyn without causing her too much fright. Then, while she was still half-asleep and her muscles were relaxed, Ruth would slip in the needle.

"I don't know how you do it," Collins told her as she was sterilizing the equipment after a shot. "She fights me, and O'Leary told me that during the day they needed three nurses just to hold her down."

"She knows that we're kindred frightened spirits," Ruth said. She said it lightly, but within herself she knew it to be true.

Perry Watts was sleeping peacefully when she looked into Room 331. There was a pile of science fiction magazines on the bed-table, and there was a little smile on his lips. In all probability, Perry Watts hadn't had such a fuss made over him in twenty years.

That morning on the way home she stopped in Mercier's Diner for coffee. She walked in without looking at anyone. But while she was sipping her hot, black brew she began to glance around casually. Nobody she knew was there. She drank three cups in all, very slowly, to allow the minutes to float by. Then, finally, she gave up and went back to her room at Mrs. Hanscom's boardinghouse. When she fell asleep she dreamed of Monterey.

Chapter Five

At first she thought it was coincidence that threw her into the company of Dr. Alden MacKenzie so often in the week that followed.

"He must have an unusually heavy load of patients on our floor," she said to Collins one night.

The other nurse looked at her and smiled. "You think so?" she said. "I think that he's making excuses to come to Revere. I also think that if he were ever to brave his mother's wrath long enough to date a nurse, he'd ask you out, Mason."

Ruth was genuinely startled. "Collins," she said, "your imagination is working overtime."

On the following day, however, she was having supper in the staff cafeteria at the hospital—to escape Mrs. Hanscom's codfish cakes, which she loathed—when Dr. MacKenzie placed his loaded tray on her table.

"May I join you?" he asked.

"Of course," she said. "I'm glad to see you, Doctor."

"Oh?" he said, obviously flattered. "I'm glad to see you, too."

"Yes," Ruth continued, "I've been wanting to ask you about young Evelyn Lambert. Are we going to run any more tests on her?"

"Oh." His face fell. "Well, she's coming right along," he said. "We'll do the usual blood smears and urinalyses. I'll come upstairs later and go over her chart with you."

"Fine," she said. There was a short pause while they both paid more attention to their food than it warranted.

"They tell me you're a stranger in Dutton," he said finally.

"Have you been inquiring?" she asked. Their eyes met, and the blunt frankness of her question at first surprised and then delighted him.

"Yes," he said. "I have. You must have a lot of free time. Would you like to meet some local people?"

She knew that he was leading up to an invitation, and she studied him. Even his hair was parted the same way as Les Simons'. It was too soon; she hadn't had enough time to find herself.

"I've met some local people, thank you, Doctor," she said crisply. She got to her feet. "I'll be expecting you on Revere Ward, then."

He smiled at her. "You'll be seeing me," he promised.

Because she was on night duty she didn't get to meet everybody at Mrs. Hanscom's. Some of the other boarders slept while she worked and worked while she slept. But Mrs. Hanscom had made it a point to introduce her to Joe Martin, the hospital pharmacist, right away. He had night duty, too.

"You can walk to work together," Mrs. Hanscom had said. "That way you'll feel safe, Ruth. Nobody's going to come running at you waving a knife with a man walking right alongside of you."

Joe Martin had beamed, but Ruth had had to struggle to keep a serious face. Joe was little and bent, a middle-aged, bald-headed man with a face like a cherub's. He was a good talker, though, and a good listener, and Ruth soon grew fond of him. They walked to work together almost every evening for several weeks.

One hot July dusk as they strolled along, Ruth grew a bit curious.

"How long have you been working nights, Joe?" she asked idly.

"Fourteen years."

The answer made her blink. "Why, that's terrible," she

36

said indignantly. "You ought to make them give you day duty once in a while."

He cackled. "I wouldn't have day duty on a platter," he said. "It would interfere with my really important work. I'm an ornithologist." He looked up at Ruth, waiting for her reaction with a proud grin on his face.

"An ornithologist?" Ruth said. "You mean you study birds?"

"Been studyin' 'em for years," Joe said. "That's why I like night work. I sleep mornings and go out during the afternoons to hunt. On my night off I even go out with a flashlight. I bet I know more about birds in Massachusetts than anybody else around. Do you like birds?"

Her knowledge of them was limited to a nodding acquaintance with a handful of California gulls and a pet canary that had died when she was eleven, but she nodded doubtfully. "Yes," she said. "I guess I do."

"Birds are just like people," Joe said. "It takes all kinds to make the world. You watch birds long enough, you get to realize that. There are honest birds like the robin, and crooked ones like the jay. There are happy birds like the flicker, and sad ones like the eagle. Did you ever notice how sad an eagle is? Proud and fierce, but sad as all get-out. That's because he's smart enough to know that, as strong as he is, the odds are against him."

Ruth laughed. This little man lived in a world she had never seen, and it was fascinating. "What's the smartest bird of all?" she asked.

"That's easy," Joe answered without hesitation. "The crow. The crow's the smartest bird that ever lived. Crows've got to be smart to keep on living. They're clumsy flyers and they don't have much in the way of hunting equipment. So they live by their brains. You know what Henry Ward Beecher once said about crows?"

"What?" Ruth could see that he enjoyed giving his lecture.

"Henry Ward Beecher once said that if men had feathers and wings, very few of them would be clever enough to be crows."

Ruth laughed. "If I had feathers and wings," she said, "what would I be?"

37

They had reached the hospital, and the question gave Joe an opportunity to leave her in style. "That's easy," he said. "A nightingale. A Florence Nightingale." He winked, then turned off down the corridor which led to the pharmacy. Ruth chuckled all the way up to Revere Ward. Joe Martin made her feel happy. It was a good way to begin the night.

It had taken four of them to shift the man from the rolling stretcher to the hospital bed. Ruth Mason looked at him as she and Collins arranged the oxygen tent. She twisted the knob on the tank and the oxygen rushed into the tent with a tortured hiss. The man groaned. He had a huge body and a face like a St. Bernard, topped by a shock of grizzled hair. His hands were cracked and grime-stained. A mechanic or a truck driver, Ruth thought. She'd have to ask him later. Right now it was impossible to ask him anything.

He was unconscious.

Dr. Anderson was giving a new intern a lesson in diagnostics. Ruth watched his square, efficient-looking hands as he moved the stethoscope over the patient's chest.

"Heartbeat is very rapid," he said.

The man's face was gray, and wet with perspiration. A muscle twitched in the corner of his mouth, and his lips were bloodless and dry.

"What do you think it is?" Dr. Anderson asked softly.

The new intern's name was Dr. Rawlings. He stared at the patient for a long moment; then he moistened his lips with his tongue.

"I'd say that this man is in diabetic coma, Doctor," he said.

"Why?" said Dr. Anderson. He picked up his stethoscope in his right hand and began to tap the knuckles of his left hand. Watching him, Ruth knew with a sudden rush of sympathy that the intern's diagnosis had been wrong.

"The color of the fingertips and earlobes, for one thing," Dr. Rawlings said. "They're blue." He raised the unconscious man's eyelids with his fingertips. "Pupils are dilated. Breathing is fast and shallow. The patient is unconscious."

"What treatment would you recommend?" Dr. Anderson said calmly.

"Insulin," the intern said. He was gaining confidence. "A dosage of . . . oh, let's see, 60 units to start, 30 intravenously and 30 subcutaneously. Would that do it?"

"Would you like to give the order?" Dr. Anderson asked.

"Yes." The intern turned toward Ruth. "Would you get the insulin, please? I'll write the order in the chart."

"I wouldn't," said Dr. Anderson—now his voice flicked like a whiplash—"because you'd be writing an order that would kill your patient."

The young doctor stared wordlessly.

"Now get this," Dr. Anderson said, "so that you never make this mistake again. That's why you're an intern, so learn the lesson the first time. Unless I'm very much mistaken, this man has had an overdose of insulin. I'm pretty sure he's in insulin shock. If he were in diabetic coma his skin would be dry; he's perspiring heavily. His pulse would be feeble instead of pronounced. His breath would smell of acetone, which it does not. I want you to run tests for sugar. If you find none, put him on intravenous glucose. When he wakes up, make him drink lots of orange juice." He turned on his heel and walked swiftly toward the elevator.

A technician hurried in to take the tests, and within minutes the diagnosis was confirmed: insulin shock. Ruth was careful not to look at Dr. Rawlings as she helped rig the intravenous bottle and fix the needle in the patient's vein.

"Boy, that's some beginning," Dr. Rawlings said. The embarrassment was thick in his voice. "That's the greatest little old beginning in the history of Memorial Hospital, I'll bet."

"The staff men don't expect interns to be right every time," Ruth said carefully. "You'll find that you'll be pretty closely supervised during the next year. As he said, that's why you're an intern."

"If I pull another boner like that," he said, "I'll never

be anything but an intern." He picked up his stethoscope and stuffed it into his pocket. "Call me when he comes out of it, will you?" he said.

Dr. MacKenzie came into the room as Dr. Rawlings was leaving. The resident paused for a moment and watched the intern walk away. "What's ailing him?" he asked. "He looks as though he just tangled with a grizzly bear and lost."

Ruth chuckled. "You're not far wrong," she said. "Dr. Anderson caught him in a wrong diagnosis."

Dr. MacKenzie grimaced. "Ouch," he said. "The poor guy. I know just how he feels. The same darn thing happened to me in my second week here. But Anderson will forget about it pretty fast. He just rubs salt into the wound for a few days so the lesson will be well learned."

"Why don't you tell Dr. Rawlings that," Ruth suggested. "I'm sure it would mean a great deal to him."

"I will," he said. He turned to go, and then he half-turned back again. "I've got tomorrow night off," he said. "I was thinking that perhaps you'd like to have dinner with me and then maybe go for a drive into the country."

A refusal was on her lips, but suddenly she wanted very much to go. She smiled at him.

"Thanks," she said. "I think I'd like that." He waved and disappeared into the corridor. Suddenly she was struck by a puzzling thought, and she hurried out of the room after him. "Hey," she said. "Dr. MacKenzie." He stopped and looked at her. "How did you know that to-morrow night was my night off, too?" she asked.

He smiled, a slow, lazy smile that creased the corners of his mouth into friendly little wrinkles. "I'll never tell," he said.

The elevator arrived and he stepped into it, grinning at her as the door slid smoothly shut, separating them. She grinned, too, as she walked back to the nurses' station. He must have checked with someone in the administrative office to see what night she was off duty.

She was still grinning when she entered the station, and Collins looked up at her and chuckled.

"You look like a very self-satisfied feline who's just gulped a very delicious singing bird," Collins said.

"I have a date with young Dr. MacKenzie tomorrow evening," Ruth announced. "And, spreader of gossip, I don't think he bothered to ask his mother if it was okay to take me out."

Collins' jaw dropped. "I can't believe it," she said. "It's just never happened before."

"For everything," Ruth said as she swept up a trayful of thermometers and started out the door, "there has to be a first time. You girls probably frightened him off every time he started to get up enough courage to ask you out." She left the station followed by a very unladylike noise coming from the general direction of Nurse Peg Collins.

It took her almost an hour to make the rounds of the ward and record the evening temperatures. When she came back to the station she found Collins waiting for her. She had a copy of the Dutton *Evening Gazette* with her.

"*You* look like a canary," Ruth told her, "who's just swallowed a cat."

"Read this," Collins told her.

It was an item in the "Social Notes" column of the society page: *Mrs. Elizabeth MacKenzie of Pool Hill will leave Dutton tomorrow to spend a week with her sister, Mrs. Roger Lardner, at the Lardner estate in Newport.*

"That," said Collins, "is why he didn't bother to ask his mother if he could take you out."

They stared at each other, and Ruth didn't know whether to laugh or get mad. She settled it by giggling, and in a second she and Collins were clinging to each other while they did their best to laugh quietly so as not to waken their sleeping patients.

He drove a black Olds convertible, two years old but very luxurious to ride along in, especially with the top down and the warm summer air streaming in over the windshield. Ruth settled back with a pleased sigh and closed her eyes.

"This is the life," she said. "No bedpans, no thermometers, no dressings to change."

He smiled. "You're not fooling anyone in this car," he

said. "I've seen the way you look at patients. You'd rather nurse than do anything else in the world, wouldn't you?"

"Sure," she admitted. "Most of us feel the same way. Don't you feel that way about being a doctor?"

The grin faded from his face. "I feel a great many things about being a doctor," he said, "and they're all mixed up."

She didn't press him to explain. She sensed that what he was talking about was a very personal thing, so she changed the subject.

"Where are we going to eat?"

"Special place," he said.

"Secret?"

"Not especially a secret. Just a very special place."

They drove for about ten minutes down a black, lampless road, and finally he turned the car onto a dirt spur and pulled to a halt in front of a long, low house with a wide porch.

"Why, we're at a farm," she said in delight.

"One of New England's nicest," he said.

When he knocked at the door, a short, red-cheeked woman with a huge bun of gray hair on her head let them in. "Hello, Bronislawa," Dr. MacKenzie said.

"Allie!" she squealed. She stood on tiptoe and kissed him on both cheeks. "Come in, come in."

A tall, old man with a clipped, white military mustache came shuffling in from the dining room, a frilly apron tied around his waist. "I wish you would bring pretty girls to eat every night, Allie," he said. "Such a Polish meal she has prepared for you! But first—a drink." From a cut-glass decanter he poured something that looked like water into four small glasses.

"No, you're wrong," Dr. MacKenzie said. "First, introductions; *then* a drink. Miss Ruth Mason—Mr. and Mrs. Stash Kwiatkowski, two old and very dear friends of mine." Ruth shook their hands and then they raised their glasses.

"Health," Stash said gravely. They drank, and for a moment Ruth thought that she had swallowed acid.

"What is it?" she gasped when she had recovered her breath. Her eyes were streaming.

"It is a very special vodka," Stash said. "I make it myself."

As soon as the fiery liquid began to course its way through her veins Ruth realized that she was ravenous. Allie MacKenzie led her into a small, candle-lit nook where a table for two was ready and waiting.

"Aren't the Kwiatkowski's going to eat with us?" Ruth asked.

"They always join me," the young doctor said, "but this is the first time I've brought a guest, and they're smart old people. They know I want you to myself."

Ruth smiled.

Within seconds, Bronislawa was carrying in hot tureens that gave off mouth-watering, pungent odors. "Tonight," she said, "you eat like a Pole." Ruth had never tasted any of the dishes with which they were served, but she loved to explore new foods and everything was delicious. There was a steaming kapusta soup, rich with chunks of cabbage; then kielbasy sausage, followed by a delicious stuffed cabbage that Bronislawa called golomki. "In the old country," Bronislawa said, "we had a saying: 'from kapusta to kielbasy to golomki.' Here you say 'from soup to nuts.' "

Dessert was a raisin-filled sweet white bread called babka, which they had with tea. "Mmmmmmm," Ruth said dreamily. "I see what you meant. This is a very special place." Stash was playing his accordion in the next room, and the candles were sputtering low. With a contented sigh, Ruth sipped the last of her tea.

As they were leaving, Stash insisted on loading the back seat with a bushel of apples and three jugs of cider. "You like cider?" he asked Ruth.

"I love it," she answered truthfully. Bronislawa shook Ruth's hand, kissed "her doctor" on the cheek, and Allie MacKenzie roared his car down the unlighted spur road. He pointed out dark shapes that loomed on either side of them.

"See these apple trees? They all belong to the Kwiatkowskis. When they came over to this country, thirty

43

years ago, they had nothing. Stash went to work as our gardener, Bronislawa as our cook. They saved for two years before they could buy their first seedlings and plant them in rented land. Today they have one of the finest orchards in the state. Make their own cider, too."

"They're wonderful," Ruth agreed. "Do you see them often?"

"As often as I can," he said.

They drove through the night, listening to soft music from the radio.

"You're getting a reputation around the hospital as a demon for work," Allie said.

"I've got a trade," Ruth answered. "Collins heard the powers that be mention that you've got a real talent for research." They laughed together.

"Do you enjoy research?" Ruth asked.

He nodded. "It's probably what I'd do later on, if there were no other factors involved," he said.

"Oh?"

"Yeah. You see, I'm going to buy out Eric Lohnes's practice when I finish my residency."

She hadn't been in Dutton long, but already the name of Dr. Lohnes was familiar to her. It was a name which owned a prominent position on the society page, and likely as not the doctor's picture would be there with it: a horse-faced man in correct tails and white tie. Dr. Lohnes was a society doctor, a specialist in piddling or nonexistent diseases which only the rich could afford. A member of one of the town's oldest families himself, he was the only medical man in Dutton who was socially acceptable to the country-club crowd. Ruth could picture what Allie MacKenzie's life would be: a few hours of prescribing sleeping pills, a couple of sociable house calls, and a great deal of entertaining.

"Your life is all measured out for you, isn't it?" she said. "A safe path to follow. You're lucky. A lot of young fellows your age are worrying about where they're going to borrow money for a shingle and some second hand office equipment."

"I wish I were, too," he said, and suddenly his voice was heavy with bitterness. He braked the convertible to

44

a sudden stop by the side of the road. "You know how I became interested in medicine?" he said. "It was on a troopship in 1944. We were torpedoed. I was just a scared infantry private, one of a gang of guys huddled on deck waiting for the ship to sink. The corpsmen and the medics needed some help, so they pulled me into the sick bay and put me to work. There was a Navy surgeon there—a short, fat guy with a big belly and a sharp nose. David Godenstern, Lieutenant (jg). I watched him cut and sew and amputate and swab and operate for thirty hours without resting. He was a little, homely man, almost ridiculous looking when you saw him later with his civilian stomach pushing out against the uniform. But do you know what he was in that sick bay?"

Ruth looked at him wordlessly.

"He was the strong arm of God. The only hope hundreds of wounded sailors and G.I.'s had of ever getting home alive. He's why I studied medicine."

She felt compelled to say it. "Was he at all like Dr. Lohnes?"

He gave a short, bitter laugh and started the car again.

"No, he wasn't like Lohnes. But you see my mother has known Lohnes for a long time, and she's never met Godenstern."

She wanted to say a lot more, but it wasn't her place to, so she kept quiet. They drove home with the pleasure gone out of the evening. At her door, Allie MacKenzie held her hand for a moment.

"I'm glad I met you, Ruth Mason," he said. "I had a good time. Will you see me next Thursday?"

She hesitated just a second. "I'd love to," she said. His mother, she thought to herself, would be home before then. Perhaps they would meet. Ruth was curious to see what kind of a woman kept her son so tightly under her thumb.

In her room upstairs, she found a note just inside the door when she switched on the light. It was in Mrs. Hanscom's spidery writing: *A young man who says his name is Gillis was here to see you. He says he will see you at the hospital tomorrow night.*

Chapter Six

Gillis arrived the next evening, looking very clean cut and gentle, despite his size.

"Hello, Sergeant," she said. She stuck out her hand and he shook it gingerly.

"I was in your neighborhood last night," he said, "and I thought that perhaps you'd like to go out for coffee."

"How's your case coming?" she asked. "Perry Watts should be going home in a day or two, I understand."

"Yeah," he said.

"You don't sound at all happy for him," she said.

"Oh, I am," he said. "He's a nice little guy. But as a witness he's strictly nothing. Perry Watts knows only one thing—he was stabbed. And we knew that without his telling us."

"Let's hope he's the last one," she said. "Maybe whoever's doing all this attacking will suddenly become sane. Maybe he'll pack up and go away."

"He won't pack up and go away," said Gillis. "And he won't suddenly become sane. He'll just wait until the urge becomes too strong for him to fight any more, and then some dark night there'll be another knifing."

She shivered.

"That isn't why I wanted to see you, though," he said. He shifted his hat from his left hand to his right. "What I said about wanting to take you out sometime—I meant it. How about making it your next night off?"

"That would be next Thursday," she said. "I'm sorry, but I have a date for Thursday evening."

His face darkened. "Sure," he said shortly. "Forget I ever mentioned it."

She saw that he misunderstood and thought that she was just putting him off again.

"No, look," she said. Her hand went out and touched his arm. "I really would like to go out with you, but I happen to have another date. Won't you call me some other time?"

He grinned a crooked grin. "I'll tell you what," he said. "Any time you're free, you give me a ring, huh?" He nodded and turned and walked away.

Ruth stared after him.

On Wednesday evening Dr. Alden MacKenzie sought her out. He made small talk for a while, and then he looked at her sheepishly. "Ruth," he said, "I hate to say this, but there's a clinic tomorrow night on surgical techniques, and the whole staff is ordered to attend. That means that our date is canceled."

She could see that he really was sorry. "Don't worry about it," she assured him. "Any nurse who expects a doctor to be able to keep an appointment is either a fool or an optimist."

He brightened when he saw that she wasn't angry. "You're a real sport, fella," he said. "Maybe next—" But before he could finish, the precise voice of the public-address operator began to page him; he was wanted in surgery. "I'll talk to you later," he said, as he hurried off.

All evening she kept away from the telephone as if it were loaded with diphtheria bacilli. On the way home the following morning she stopped in the diner, but Gillis wasn't there. On sudden impulse she stepped into a phone booth and looked up the local number of the Massachusetts State Police. When she dialed the number a fresh, crisp voice answered after the first ring.

"State Police, Corporal Zamborski."

"May I speak to Sergeant Gillis?" she asked.

There was a pause. "One moment, please." She could hear his voice on the other end of the line. "Sarge," he shouted, "it's a girl."

When Gillis came to the phone he sounded a little embarrassed. "Hello?"

"It's Ruth," she said, "Ruth Mason. My date for tonight was called off; you said to call you when I was free."

"Do you mean it?" he said. He no longer sounded embarrassed; he sounded happy. Then he started to laugh. She had never heard him laugh like that before, and even over the telephone it was a very nice sound. "I'll call for you at eight-thirty," he said. "Will that be okay?"

"That will be just fine," she said.

"Ruth," he said. "I want to say one more thing. . . ."

"Yes?"

"Thanks for calling."

He had borrowed a car. It was old and it wasn't a convertible, but all the windows were rolled down open.

"What'll we do?" he asked. "Dinner now or later? How about a drive-in movie?"

"Anything you say," Ruth told him. "I sleep so late that I don't usually have dinner until shortly before I go on duty. I'll be satisfied just to ride and talk."

"I know," he said. "Want to do something different?"

Not another Polish meal in a farmhouse, she told herself. Massachusetts men, it seemed, like to make their dates interesting. "What do you have in mind?" she asked.

"Ever been to a night court?"

She hadn't, and they went. The courthouse was a big, dark building that smelled of old leather bindings and musty decisions. There was a winding, stone staircase, and on the second floor Gillis led her into a room with swinging doors marked "Courtroom B." The guard nodded familiarly.

"Hi, Sarge," he whispered. Court was in session.

They settled down into leather-upholstered chairs and watched the proceedings. From time to time Ruth noticed Gillis watching her face.

It was a pathetic procession of broken men that came before the night-court judge. Drunkards, brawlers, addicts and petty thieves waited their turns to shuffle up before the bench, tell their stories and receive their jail sentences. Ruth watched for about ten minutes, and then she turned a white face toward Gillis.

"Please," she said. "Take me out of here."

He didn't say anything until they were out in the street and he was leading her toward the car. "Are you all right?" he asked anxiously. She nodded, and he sighed in relief.

He drove in silence for a while.

"Why did you take me there?" she asked.

"It was sort of a test," he said. "I give it to most of the girls I take out."

"A test?" For a moment she felt a puzzled anger. What right did he have to test her or any other girl? "You mean I failed," she said. "Showed that I didn't have the nerve to watch all that misery back there?" She felt her face go hot with fury.

"I mean," he said quietly, "that you passed. Nothing about a cop's job is fun. Seeing 'all that misery back there' is just as tough on us as it was on you. Some people go to night court and laugh. I'm glad you didn't."

For a moment she stared at him, speechless. "You're a very complicated man, Detective-Sergeant Gillis," she said finally.

He drove onto Route 9 and followed the flow of the traffic for about twenty minutes, and then he pulled into a driveway. It was a small place, but there was a good number of cars in the tiny lot. There was a simple neon sign: THE WRECK'S.

Inside, the air was full of the smell of good food. They made their way to a booth near the piano. Several of the diners nodded to Ed Gillis.

"Does everybody in the state know you?" she asked.

He grinned, but she could see that he was pleased. "I come here a lot," he said. When they were seated he ordered steaks and onion rings. There were salt sticks in a basket on the table, and they munched while they listened to the music.

The man at the piano had skin the color of ebony. He was big, bigger even than Ed Gillis. His hair was a white cap. He swayed to and fro to the saddest tinkling piano Ruth had ever heard, and he poured his voice over the music like a rich syrup. Ruth had never heard the song before.

"What's it called?" she whispered.

Ed smiled. "It hasn't got a name. None of The Wreck's songs have names. He makes them up as he goes along. They're never the same twice."

When the song was over the man got up and left the piano. He started to walk past their booth.

"Wreck," Ed said softly.

Instantly the big man turned toward them with a smile and stuck out his hand.

"Hello, Detective," he said. "Everything all right?"

"Everything's fine," Ed Gillis answered. "I want you to meet a friend."

"Man friend or lady friend?" The Wreck asked. It seemed like an odd reply to Ruth, and she looked at the man sharply. Then she noticed his eyes. They were dull and half closed, staring ahead at nothing.

He was blind.

"Lady friend," Ed Gillis said. "Ruth Mason, The Wreck—king of the real blues this side of New Orleans."

The Wreck chuckled. He stuck out his hand and Ruth let her own be enveloped by it.

"How do you do?" she said.

"I do just fine," he said. "Our friend Gillis here makes me feel good. He knows how to say nice things. It's part of what makes him a popular policeman."

He grinned in Gillis' direction. "I got a question for you, popular policeman. You know Seth? My boy?"

"Sure I do," Ed said. "Not in trouble, I hope."

The Wreck showed white teeth. "Nothin' like that from Seth. But he wants a .22 rifle so he can hunt the woods around here. What do you think? I'm a little afraid of the combination of a kid and a rifle."

"Give it to him," Gillis said. "You know he's a good, responsible kid. Give it to him, preach him a little safety lecture, and turn him loose to enjoy himself."

"That's about the way I had it figured," The Wreck said, "but it makes me happy to hear you say it." He stared sightlessly in Ruth's direction and smiled. "I'll be leavin' you now 'cause I don't want to get to be feelin' too happy. Get too happy, can't feel blue enough to sing the blues." He chuckled again, then he walked away.

They watched him thread a passage across the crowded room.

"He used to be a wrestler," Ed Gillis said. "A good one. Earned good money, until one day he was thrown across the ring and he hit his head on a post. When he woke up, he was blind. He used to sing blues because he loved to. Then he started to sing for a living. He has a brother who's a great cook, and the two of them finally decided to open a spot. I come here all the time. So do a lot of other people."

Their steaks arrived, and the sirloins were just right, black on the outside and pink and juicy under the charcoal-broiled crust. They both ate hungrily, and Ruth did full justice to her steak.

"You have a lot of appetite," Ed grinned. It was a compliment rather than a jibe, and Ruth took it in the spirit in which it was given.

"You leave a pretty clean plate yourself," she said. They were enjoying apple pie and coffee and listening to The Wreck's beautiful blues when the state trooper came into the room. Ruth watched him as he moved from table to table.

"You should have stayed in uniform," she said. "It's a nice, smart uniform. I'll bet you look great in it." He smiled at her. An answer was on his lips, but he followed her gaze, and when he saw the trooper the grin faded from his face.

"Bates," he called.

The trooper came over at once. "I had a feeling you'd be here," he said. "I've been looking all over for you. They want you back in Dutton right away."

Ruth and Ed got to their feet. Gillis dropped a bill on the table and they headed for the door. "What's up?" Gillis asked.

The Wreck was singing a dirge with no name, and Ruth had to listen hard to hear the trooper's answer; but she heard it, and her stomach knotted in sudden fear.

"They found another guy on the sidewalk."

"Same thing?" Gillis asked.

The trooper nodded. "Knifed in the back," he said.

Chapter Seven

Young Evelyn Lambert pushed the wagon laden with charts, little glasses containing capsules and pills, and thermometers that bristled from alcohol-filled tumblers.

"Only half an hour tonight, Mason," she said professionally. "That isn't too bad, but I still think we take their temps too often."

Ruth tried not to grin. She knew that the girl waited all day long just so she could wheel the cart for her in the evening. Evelyn had confided that she was going to become a nurse, too, when she grew a little older. She studied the mannerisms of all the nurses in the hospital and copied them, even following the professional practice of calling them by their last names.

"Orders are orders, Lambert," Ruth said. She rumpled the girl's hair. "Now off to bed with you."

"Can I read a little?" Evelyn asked. Ruth looked at her fondly. Room 318 would be getting a new occupant soon. She didn't look like the same frightened child she had been when Ruth first came to Memorial Hospital. She had gained weight, her face had color, and her eyes were bright. The Proteus microbe that had been setting up colonies in her kidneys had decided that it was silly to argue with a formidable foe like streptomycin, and it was almost out of her system.

"No reading tonight," Ruth said firmly. "If you keep up the good work we'll be saying 'so long' to you one of these days soon, and we don't want to spoil things now. You can listen to the radio, though. Play it softly, and I'll come in and turn it off after you fall asleep."

Collins was sterilizing a syringe in the nurses' station. "How's that boy who was stabbed?" she asked.

"I haven't been able to find out," Ruth said. "They've got him in a private room on the sixth floor. The police couldn't question him last night; he was getting blood transfusions."

"Boy," Collins said, "I don't mind telling you that here is one girl who is terrified. I used to walk to work from the house—it's only two blocks. But from here on until they catch that character, I'm taking the bus right to the hospital door."

"That's just as bad," Ruth pointed out. "Hanging around a lonely bus stop late at night isn't exactly giving you maximum security." They looked at each other, and Collins shivered.

Ed Gillis came into the ward shortly before midnight.

"Hi," he said. "I didn't have a chance to tell you last night. I had a good time." He looked haggard and tired, and there was a blue stubble of whiskers on his square chin.

"I had a good time too," she said. "Until we got the news."

He nodded.

"How is he?" she asked.

"He'll be okay," Gillis said. "I talked with him for a while this afternoon, and checked on him again just now. He's a fifteen-year-old kid named Leon Goldstein. He was coming home from a movie, crossing a vacant lot. Two young girls found him and called the police."

"Did he see the man who attacked him?"

"No. The usual thing, he was knifed in the back. But we did get one break."

"What was that?" Ruth asked.

"He saw the man's shoes," Ed said. "Just before he lost consciousness, the man who had attacked him came over and stood for a second by his head. The kid saw his shoes."

"Will that help?" Ruth asked.

"They were white shoes," Ed said slowly. "It may help. We can narrow our search down to the kind of man who wears them. They're not considered too stylish any more by anyone but a college boy."

Ruth sighed. "It doesn't seem to me that that's too big a help," she said. "It still could be any one of thousands of men in Dutton."

"Every little break counts in this business," Ed said grimly. "There's another possibility. He may be someone whose duties call for him to wear white shoes. A hospital employee, perhaps even a doctor."

"Oh, I don't think he's a doctor," Ruth protested. "Why, a doctor would have to be crazy to . . ." Her voice dwindled off.

Ed nodded grimly. "Exactly," he said. "You don't think we're dealing with a sane man, do you?" He put a hand on her elbow. "Ruth, I want you to promise me that you'll be very careful from now on. Do you realize why every one of the people who've been attacked has been brought to Memorial Hospital?"

She was puzzled. "No," she said. "I never stopped to wonder why."

"Because, so far," Ed said, "every attack has taken place in the vicinity of Memorial. This doesn't mean that he may not strike somewhere else in the future, but it does make me almost certain that this guy spends his life, day to day, within a few blocks of where we're standing right now."

A light outside a room far down the hall began to flash. "I'll be careful, Ed," she promised hurriedly.

"I'll be watching out for you as much as I can," he said softly. He stood and stared while she hurried down the dark corridor. Then, while he waited for the elevator he took out a cigarette and placed it between his lips.

He drove halfway to the State Police barracks before he remembered to light it.

Gillis was a slow and cautious man, she decided. Either that, or his case was keeping him very busy, because he didn't call her on the following day, or during the three days that followed.

Allie MacKenzie, however, moved into her life with cheerful confidence. He telephoned her at Mrs. Hanscom's at odd hours; visited her while she was on duty and plied her and Collins with gifts of chocolate bars, which they greedily accepted; and otherwise played the role of the infatuated young man.

54

On Tuesday he invited her to have tea with his mother on the following afternoon. Filled with a sort of curious dread, Ruth went with him on Wednesday to a big, old, New England house on exclusive Pool Hill. She was welcomed on the terrace by a warm, middle-aged woman.

Elizabeth MacKenzie was short and plump, with ash-gray hair. Ruth had half expected to find her wearing a severe black dress, and sporting pince-nez; but she wore a smartly cut summer suit, and, although she wore eyeglasses, they were horn-rimmed.

"Welcome, Miss Mason," she said when Allie introduced them. "I've heard a lot about you."

"And I about you," Ruth said. For a moment they measured one another in the manner of women since time began, and each grudgingly had to admit to herself that the first impression was good. They had tea on the terrace, cooled by a breeze that skipped over the city below and snobbishly spread its comfort on the hill, as if conscious that the moneyed individuals of Dutton lived there.

A manservant in a white jacket served tiny cucumber sandwiches with the iced tea and cookies, and Ruth felt like a character in an English play. She watched Allie thoughtfully. He was as much at ease here as he was in the hospital. She had always known about his money, but she had never imagined the life he led on account of it.

He caught her looking at him. "Do you play tennis?" he asked. "We have a good cork court, and no one ever uses it. I love to play."

"I do, too," Ruth said. "But it's been a long time since I have." She realized with surprise that the last time she had played had been with Les Simons. The thought didn't hurt at all. She had been too busy and happy in the past few weeks to brood. The wound he had inflicted had healed fast; Les Simons had no place in her life any more. The ability to think of him so calmly suddenly struck her as the most amusing thing that had ever happened to her, and she smiled.

55

"How about a game right now?" Allie said. "We should have spare clothes and things around somewhere. I know we have extra rackets."

"Swell," Ruth said.

"I'll go get everything," Allie said. "You two just sit and relax until I get back. Save your strength, Ruth. I'm going to run you ragged."

"We'll see," Ruth said. She had once played a strong game, and she knew she would probably be able to make him earn his points. She watched him run along the flagstone path toward the house.

"My son likes you very much," Elizabeth MacKenzie said.

Ruth looked at her. "I'm glad," she said. "I like Allie, too."

"He could do more than like you," Elizabeth said. "He's very close to falling in love with you. I have never seen him so impressed with a girl."

Ruth stared. "Why are you telling me this?" she asked.

The glasses tinkled as Elizabeth refilled them with iced tea.

"I think from what I've seen of you that you would probably make any man an admirable wife," she said. "But you would ruin my plans for Alden."

Ruth felt the blood climb to her face. Behind the horn-rimmed glasses, Elizabeth MacKenzie's small blue eyes were watchful.

"It's become unfashionable to consider social leadership a duty," the older woman said, "but I prefer to consider it a very important one. There has been a MacKenzie fulfilling that duty in Dutton for almost two hundred years. Next year, when Alden has left the hospital, there will be three important organizational positions waiting for him. The following year will see more of the same coming his way. To help him fulfill these obligations he needs a wife with family, social heritage. This isn't mere snobbery; it's fact."

Ruth sipped her tea for a moment and tried to regain her composure. "Mrs. MacKenzie," she said carefully, "I feel that my relationship with Allie is a very personal thing."

56

Elizabeth MacKenzie smiled at her warmly. "But I am his mother," she said.

"Mrs. MacKenzie," Ruth said bluntly, "you are not my mother."

The other woman's smile faded swiftly. "You feel insulted," she said. "I can understand that."

"My feelings have nothing to do with what I am saying," Ruth said. "I think, since you have set the frank tone of this conversation, that I should tell you that you are doing your son's career great harm. Allie has a fine, inquiring, medical mind. Important men on the hospital staff feel that he could make a real contribution in medical research some day. Don't you think that kind of work would be more important than taking over Dr. Lohnes's practice of neurotic rich women, and leading the cotillion at civic balls?"

Elizabeth sighed heavily. "We look at the world, my dear," she said, "through different pairs of eyes."

"We do," Ruth agreed quietly.

"Last year," Elizabeth said, "Allie had another one of his reckless impulses. He was going to apply for a fellowship from the American Cancer Society, and go and close himself up in a stuffy little laboratory in New York City."

"Why didn't he?" Ruth said.

"Because I made him see that it would have been a mistake," Elizabeth said in the patient voice of an adult talking to a child. "In the first place, although some people think he should be ashamed of it, he's a pretty well-off young man. He doesn't need fellowships."

"All your money, Mrs. MacKenzie," Ruth said in the same patient tone, "couldn't buy Allie the research facilities of the American Cancer Society."

"And in the second place," Elizabeth said, "I thought it would be a step in the wrong direction."

Ruth felt a retort hot and bitter on her tongue, but she swallowed it and said nothing. It was, she reminded herself, really none of her business. She sipped her tea.

When Allie came back he found the two women sitting and chatting amicably about the latest recordings of the Boston Symphony. A few minutes later, having changed into tennis things, Ruth stood on the fine cork court and smacked the ball over the net. Allie returned it in a long, shallow drive that told her he was good. She thought of his mother as she drove it back to him with a vicious forehand smash that sent the ball over like a bullet. From the sidelines, Elizabeth MacKenzie called out in a complacent, motherly tone.

"Don't play too long, children," she said. "The sun is hot."

The summer had moved along swiftly, the days dropping away one by one. She was too busy to feel the drag of time. The hospital was full, and her working shift went fast. Her social life was full, too, with both Gillis and Allie MacKenzie claiming her attention as often as they were able to find her free from duty. One Thursday afternoon early in August, however, she awoke to find that she was off duty that evening and without a date. Allie had an operation to observe, and Gillis was in Boston on State Police business.

On her way down to eat, Joe Martin hailed her with a cheery hello.

"It's a beautiful day out," he told her. "It's a sin to stay inside on a day like today. Why don't you come along with me this afternoon into the woods, and I'll show you some of the most beautiful little feathered creatures in creation."

He had made the offer before, but Ruth had never taken him seriously. Now, however, the thought of being out in the woods was too tempting to pass up.

"Give me five minutes to get into something sensible," she told him, "and you've got yourself a fellow bird-watcher."

She put on slacks, low-heeled shoes, and a jersey, and as an afterthought she knotted a cardigan sweater around her neck by the sleeves. Joe Martin's face lighted up when he saw her.

"By the great, jumpin' horned toad," he said, "I haven't had a prettier date in the last forty years."

"You tell that to all your dates," Ruth said with a grin.

Mrs. Hanscom was in the kitchen, and Ruth obtained permission to make two picnic lunches, which she packed in a shoebox and tied with twine. Joe Martin carried it. "I travel light," he said. He had no equipment except a pair of binoculars slung around his neck, and a notebook and pencil-stub in his pocket. They took a bus to the end of the line; Ruth had Joe open the window so she could enjoy the ride, letting the air rush in and whip about her face like a fresh Monterey wave. When they got off the bus she let Joe lead. He left the road almost at once and struck out across country, cutting through a couple of rolling farm meadows until he came to the woods. He knew the country intimately—Ruth could see that.

"You walk these trails as if they were city blocks," she said.

"I ought to," Joe said. "I was walking some of them when they weren't even trails."

Suddenly he stopped and held up his hand. "Hear it?" he whispered.

Ruth hadn't; but then the bird trilled again, a rich, throaty stream of notes coming from the foliage of a tree not far ahead. Moving slowly, Joe handed her the lunch-box and picked up the binoculars. In a few moments he gave a grunt of satisfaction. Wordlessly, he handed her the glasses and pointed. For a couple of seconds she had trouble seeing; but then she adjusted the lenses and it sprang into life before her eyes: a small black and brown bird with wing-tips of pure, clean white.

"A male oriole," Joe whispered. "Unless I'm mistaken, the female should be somewhere around here in a nest." They started to walk slowly, while Joe's eyes searched the trees overhead. "There it is." Again Ruth had trouble finding it, but finally she saw it, too.

Joe looked at her doubtfully. "Can you climb a tree?" he asked.

She was stung into daring by his tone. "I was the best tree climber in the state, back in California," she said.

It was an oak, and luckily it had very low branches. Once she got onto the first branch it was like climbing a leafy ladder. Joe was a lot more supple than his frail frame suggested. He swung up after her with the agility of a monkey. She was afraid to look down, but, once they came to the nest, she forgot all about fear.

"Easy now," Joe whispered. "If she's at home, we don't want to frighten her too much." But the female was gone. The nest wasn't empty, though. There were four eggs at the soft bottom of the deep bag of twigs and straw. Ruth stared at them. They were speckled, white and pink.

"Don't handle them a lot," Joe warned, "or the mother won't sit on them when she gets back. But touch one gently with your fingertip." She did, and it was warm with the heat of the female bird's body.

"Why, they have their own little maternity ward, right here," Ruth said.

"That's exactly it," said Joe. He started down, and she followed slowly. On the ground again, they waited for a few minutes; soon the mother bird, colored green and yellow, flew back and settled into the sacklike nest. Satisfied that all was well with the oriole family, Ruth and Joe walked on.

"I'll bring you back here in a couple of weeks," Joe promised. "By then we should be able to see the little ones just growing their first feathers."

Through Joe's trained eyes, Ruth saw birds in places she never would have looked, had she been alone. They hiked over miles of woodland, and by the time the shadows began to grow long, she was tired and hungry. They stopped in a little clearing by a cold, clear spring that bubbled out of a crack in a rock. Ruth opened the shoebox, and in famished silence they devoured hard-boiled eggs, roast-beef sandwiches, pickles, and cookies; then each had a drink of the icy spring water. Ruth leaned against the trunk of a tree.

"This," she said comfortably, "is the life for me. I think I'll find a cave in these woods and set up light housekeeping."

Joe Martin smiled. He had a sweet smile, like a child's. "These woods are pretty tame, now. Just a few rabbits and a deer or two. But I can remember when we had bear here."

She sat up quickly and looked around, and he chuckled. "Oh, there ain't any around here any more. Haven't been for years."

Ruth chuckled sheepishly. "You've been in Dutton for a long time, haven't you, Joe?" she said as she settled back against the tree again.

"All my life."

"My mother used to live here when she was a girl," she said.

"What was her name?"

"Lee-Ann Miller. She lived with her aunt, a Mrs. Dave Miller. Her uncle was a grocer, I think."

He sat up excitedly. "Why, child, I knew your mother," he said. "I took Lee-Ann Miller out more than once or twice."

"You really mean it?"

Joe stared at her intently. "She was smaller than you are. Darker, too. A real active girl, full of pep." He put his hand on Ruth's arm and laughed shakily. "Why, girl," he said, "if things had gone a little differently, I might have been your father." The smile faded from his face. "She isn't alive any more, is she?"

"No," Ruth said. "Both she and my father were killed in an automobile accident years ago."

Joe sighed. "I knew it," he said, "from the way you talked." For a moment, neither said anything. "Your father," Joe asked. "Would he be the young West Pointer who rushed her away before I even got started with my own slow-poke courting?"

"He was an Army man," Ruth smiled.

"Yes," Joe said, "I remember him, too. Well, that was a long time ago."

For a few minutes they sat in the little clearing in the woods, each busy with his own thoughts. Through Joe's memory of them, Ruth felt closer to her parents than she had in years. Finally, however, Joe got to his feet with a sigh.

"We'd better be getting back," he said. "I'm on duty tonight in the pharmacy." They cleaned up the clearing, and then they walked over another forest trail in the fading afternoon.

"Got a date tonight?" Joe asked affably.

"No," Ruth laughed. "I'm just unpopular, I guess. Nobody asked me."

61

"That's not the way I heard it," Joe said. "Wouldn't even have to listen to hospital gossip. I saw young Doc MacKenzie looking at you the other day. Now there's a lad who wouldn't sit around while a West Pointer walked off with his girl."

"Allie's very nice," Ruth said. Reticent by nature, she hated to discuss her personal feelings with people who weren't intimates. Joe Martin seemed to sense this. He glanced at her sharply.

"Might say that it was none of my business. Might be right, too. But I knew your mother pretty well, and I thought a lot of her. So I'd like to give you some advice. I've known Allie MacKenzie since he was old enough to break windows. He's a fine boy, Ruth. Fine family. Lots of money. He'll make a good doctor. And a good husband for some lucky girl."

Ruth felt the blood climb into her face. "I've known Allie only a couple of months," she said. "I have lots of friends."

Again the old man looked at her sharply. "I heard about one of them friends," he said. "You've been seeing that state cop, haven't you?"

"Ed Gillis," she said. "Yes, I have."

Joe sniffed. "Everyone to his own taste," he said.

This time Ruth showed her anger. "Ed Gillis," she said, "is a friend of mine. And I see no reason to have to account to anyone in this world for the people I choose to see."

Immediately Joe looked ashamed. "You're absolutely right, girl," he said. "Gillis is probably okay, too. It's just that he came down to the hospital last week and asked all of us a lot of silly questions. Oh, I know," he said, anticipating Ruth's protest, "he was just doing his job. But none of the local cops works that way. These state cops, they have to make so many arrests a week to make good. They figure everybody they talk to is hiding something."

"I think you're mistaken," Ruth said quietly.

Joe patted her on the shoulder. "I understand," he said. "Believe me, I hope I'm mistaken, too."

They broke free of the forest and entered a meadow. On the far side of it was a long stretch of apple orchard, and something about the cluster of farm buildings near-by tugged at her memory.

"Is this the Kwiatkowski place?" she asked.

"Sure is," Joe said. "You know them?"

"Yes." Just then she saw Stash and Bronislawa, standing next to a truck that was being loaded with crates full of apples. "Hi!" she shouted. They waved back, and she and Joe walked toward them.

"Miss Mason!" Bronislawa said. "You come back for more golomki?"

"Any time," Ruth said. "But today we've just been enjoying ourselves."

"Bird-watching, eh?" said Stash. He and Joe grinned at one another. Evidently they had known each other for a long time. "You had nice day for it."

"Oh, it's been a beautiful day," said Ruth. "It still is lovely out. I hate to go back to the city."

"You work tonight?" Stash asked.

"No, I'm off."

"I have to drive my own truck into city at midnight with load apples," he said. "Why not stay here and drive in with me?"

"Oh, that will be just fine," Ruth said.

Joe Martin looked as if he would have liked to stay too, but he said his good-by's. "It's back to pill-rolling for me," he said. He squeezed Ruth's hand. "You're not mad at an old fool for shooting off his mouth, are you?"

She had been, but he looked so unhappy that all her anger melted away.

"No, Joe," she said. "Thanks for giving me a good time." He smiled, then he turned away and started for the road and the long bus ride back to town.

Bronislawa seemed happy to see her again. "You want me to show you our apple farm?" she said. Ruth agreed eagerly. Soon she was being ushered through wide, low sheds where long rows of apple crates were being packed with red and yellow fruit.

"The yellow ones are Transparents," Bronislawa explained. "The reds are Astrachans. These are the first of the season. Later come Baldwins. I like Baldwins best."

63

Men and girls worked busily over the crates, sorting the apples for size and quality. The soft ones and the bad drops were tossed into large bins, which would later be sorted and emptied into the cider press. Ruth inhaled. The shed gave forth an aroma which was a mixture of fresh paint and label glue and the winey smell of early apples.

Bronislawa selected four choice apples carefully and stuffed them into the pockets of Ruth's cardigan. Outside the shed, they walked a little way into the orchard. The trees, heavy with fruit and leaves, formed corridors which seemed to stretch endlessly into the distance.

"You must have work to do," Ruth said.

"Well . . ." Bronislawa seemed torn between duty and hospitality.

"Go ahead. I'll just take a walk and enjoy myself. I'll be back in a couple of hours."

"Don't get lost," Bronislawa said anxiously.

"Don't worry," Ruth laughed. "I won't go far."

She walked across a meadow, the apples in the sweater bumping against her hip. The cool air felt good on her face. She started to climb a wooded hill, walking slowly, savoring the falling dusk. She loved this part of the day best of all. Colors began to fade from the world; everything became some shade of grayish blue. She climbed a low stone wall and walked faster until she reached the crest of the hill; then she sank down on the grass under a tree.

She felt tired, and the grass was soft beneath her body. She pulled a handful of the green shoots and let the breeze blow them from her palm, a few blades at a time.

Her mind was a jumble of questions set off by Joe Martin's rambling monologue. Was Allie really in love with her? Was Gillis the duty-driven man she believed him to be, or was he, as Joe had hinted, just a brutal cop? The grass on which she lay seemed to her the softest and greenest she had ever seen.

"Loaf with me on the grass," she murmured aloud. It was a line she had had to memorize at Monterey High. She felt drowsy. She slept.

When she awoke, her first impression was that all of

Dutton stretched out before her. Darkness had almost completely fallen, and electric lights began to pop on and off. Now here. Now there. It was as if the rays of the moon were reflected on a giant tinsel which glittered back points of its light.

Ruth shivered a little; she took the cardigan from around her neck and put it on. Then she reached into her pocket and took out an apple. She rubbed it vigorously against her sweater and then bit into it. The apple crackled as her teeth pierced the firm skin, and the tart juice ran and dripped off her fingers. She chewed the sweet Transparent, not thinking of anything, becoming part of the world which lay silent and dark around her.

Chapter Eight

All night long the heat had made sleep impossible. Moist and miserable, Ruth lay on her boardinghouse bed and thought of the cool Pacific. Her window was open and the curtains were drawn back, but not a breath of air entered the room or stirred outside.

She waited until the sun rose, and then, wilted and puffy-eyed, she telephoned Peg Collins.

"Can you sleep?" she asked.

"Not a wink," Collins replied. "It's too hot to breathe."

"Let's go swimming," Ruth suggested.

"It's an idea," Collins said. "Pick me up down here. My place is on the way to the lake."

By seven-thirty, in slacks and jerseys, and carrying their bathing suits wrapped in towels, the girls got off a bus at Lake Dutton. Ruth looked at the water greedily. It wasn't the Pacific, but it was still a lot of wetness. Shaped almost like a river, one-quarter of a mile wide and eight miles long, the lake was flung, like a blue-green ribbon, the length of Dutton Valley.

They broke records changing their clothes, and in almost no time they were dashing into the water. At first it was so warm that Ruth almost shouted in disappointment. But then, as her body cut the surface and she began to swim under water, jackknifing her long legs in powerful thrusts that kept her close to the bottom, she began to feel the chill of the depths. It was a cold, green world, and, in contrast to the blazing heat of the one above the surface, it was delightful. Schools of fish, kept below by the tepid heat of the shallow waters, stared at her fearfully as she glided by. Finally, lungs ready to burst, she pushed against the rocky bottom with the soles of her feet and shot surfaceward.

She saw, as she shook the water from her eyes, that she had swum far out from shore.

"Hey," she shouted, waving an arm at Peg as she trod water. Peg was standing near the shore, and when she saw Ruth she jumped in and began to swim toward her, using a ragged sort of dogpaddle that had carried her only a few yards when Ruth's strong crawl brought them face to face.

"Ruth Mason," Peg gasped, "don't you ever, ever do that to me again. I was frantic. I didn't know what had happened to you."

"I'm sorry," Ruth grinned. "It's been so long since I've been in, I just had to enjoy it."

They clambered up onto the beach and stood dripping in the hot sun. For that hour of the morning, the lake shore was crowded.

"It looks as if nobody in town could sleep last night," Peg said, pointing to scores of prone figures. Having come to the lake sleepless, they were catching cat-naps after cooling themselves in the water.

"Seems like a fine idea to me," Ruth said. She flopped down on the sand, and Peg sank down beside her. Neither of them tried to make conversation. Within minutes, both were fast asleep, lulled by the sun and the sound of the water lapping at the lake's edge.

Ruth was awakened by a raindrop, large as a silver dollar and icy cold, which hit her in the ankle. She blinked her eyes at the dark sky and gasped.

"Peg," she said. She shook the other girl's shoulder, waking her. "What time is it?"

There was a clock in the bathhouse tower, and by it they saw that they had napped only half an hour.

"For a moment," Ruth laughed, "I thought we had slept right through the day. Look at that sky!" Black, greasy clouds hung above them. As they studied the thunderheads, a flash of lightning shivered the air, and the thunderclap that followed made their ears ring.

"Come on," Peg shouted. "We'd better change and get out of here, before it starts to pour."

By the time they had gone into the bathhouse and had changed back into their slack outfits, it was pelting, but it wasn't rain that fell from the leaden sky. It was hail. Ruth stuck her hand out of the doorway and drew it back with an exclamation of pain. Some of the hailstones were as large as grapes, and they stung when they struck.

"Have you ever in your life seen anything like this?" Peg shouted. She was grinning with almost childish enjoyment. "Hail, this time of the year!"

But Ruth didn't grin back. She was studying the sky anxiously. "I don't like it," she said. "I've heard about things like this."

The hail stopped as suddenly as it had begun, and the air was suddenly cold and clammy. Persons who had been complaining about the heat twenty minutes earlier, now began to shiver and break out in goose bumps.

"Let's not wait for the bus," Ruth said. "There's a cab. Let's grab it."

Peg nodded in agreement, and the two girls raced for the taxi.

"Are you taken?" Ruth asked.

The cabbie didn't open the door for them. "Nope," he said.

They got in. "We're going a few blocks beyond Memorial Hospital," Ruth said.

"Okay," the cabbie said. The voice was vaguely familiar, and Ruth stared at the back of his head. He made no move to start the cab, and Ruth felt a stir of impatience.

"Are you waiting for something?" she asked.

"Someone, lady, someone," he corrected. He turned, and she knew immediately where she had seen him. He was the disagreeable driver who had taken her from the railroad station to Mrs. Hanscom's on the day of her arrival in Dutton. She read the license on the taxi panel-board. His name was Gerry Jancowski. He looked at her without recognition. "I'm the only driver for miles around, lady, and I'm not moving this heap without a full pay-load. You'll have to share the cab. If you don't like it, you can wait for the bus."

Ruth glanced at the license again, memorizing the name. It would be a pleasure, she thought, to report him. She looked out. Nobody seemed to be coming their way. "And if we have to wait half an hour for your load?" she asked.

The driver looked bored. "Then we wait," he said.

"Come on, Peg," she said. "I can't see this at all." She started to get out, but just then thunder shook the world.

"I don't know, Ruth," Peg said faintly. "We're liable to get caught right in the middle of this thing."

Ruth was looking at her in exasperation when a familiar voice reached her ears.

"Hey, Nurse! Can I save you a taxi fare?" Ed Gillis, at the wheel of a smart, gray, Massachusetts State Police squad car, had pulled to a halt on the other side of the road.

"Can you!" Ruth said. "Come on, Peg, before he changes his mind." Without a glance at the taxi driver, they changed vehicles. Ed pulled his car away with a purr of automatic gears shifting smoothly.

"I was just coming back from Boston on police business," Ed said. "I figured I could give a lift to somebody stranded in the storm, but I never figured on it being you two."

"A friend in need," Ruth said. "Believe me!" She was about to tell him about the churlish driver, when they topped the crest of a hill and Ed spoke softly.

"Do you see what I see?" He braked the car to a halt and the three of them sat there, staring through the windshield of the squad car at the city below them, and at the purple cloud which hovered over the northern end of Dutton. The cloud roiled and changed shape before their eyes, a seething, turbulent mass of air and water. From its underside drooped something that looked like a long rope. As they watched, the rope thickened and fattened until it was a cable and then a funnel. Before their eyes, it broke away from the parent cloud and, whirling and shimmying, began to move off toward the west.

"We've just watched a tornado being born," Ed said.

Ruth felt her palms begin to sweat. "What's in its path?" she asked.

"I don't know the city," Gillis said. "What's over there, Peg?"

"Where?" Peg asked. "I think . . . yes. Oh, glory, it's Valleybrook, the veterans' housing project."

"Oh, no. . . ." Ruth whispered.

Even as they watched, they could see buildings crumbling and debris being sucked up into the moving, gray funnel.

"That place is loaded with women and children," Peg cried.

"We'd better go, Ed," Ruth said quietly. "They'll be needing us."

He lurched the squad car away, tripping the siren switch as he pressed his foot down on the accelerator. For a moment the sound of the siren floated before them, loud and clear, but then, as they descended the hill, the car was buffeted by winds so strong that the mechanical scream was whipped away from them and only the roar of the wind filled their ears. The car rocked from side to side, and Ed muttered to himself as he fought to hold the wheel.

"Look at that bus," Peg shouted.

It had been overturned. The wheels were still spinning. Instinctively Ed braked to a halt, but Ruth put her hand on his arm.

"They have plenty of help," she said. It was true. They were in a business district, and men and women poured from the shops to go to the aid of the bus passengers.

"The veterans' project could be bad," she said. "Really bad. You'd better go there."

He shot the car off without bothering to reply. The rain had started again, and the downpour became torrential. The water slowed the car's progress, and Ruth steeled herself for what might lie ahead.

It was a good thing that she did.

When they got there, what met their eyes was chaos. The housing project had been constructed of reinforced concrete, but much of it had been reduced to rubble. Some of the buildings looked as if a giant hand had swiped at them, knocking off whole stories. On the top floor of one building, the roof and walls were gone, but some freak of nature had caused the tornado to leave the furniture intact. On the ground, men had already formed into rescue gangs; they dug and heaved at the rubble, looking for bodies and survivors. Passing cars and trucks were being stopped and commandeered as emergency ambulances.

Ed closed his eyes. "I've fought all the way through Europe, and again in Korea," he said, "but this is as bad a sight as I've seen." He shook his head as if to clear it, and then his instinct for action asserted itself. "Come on," he said. "Let's get to work."

They split up as soon as they left the car. Ed stripped off his suit coat and joined a group of men tugging at what remained of a wall. From beneath the mortar and plaster, Ruth could hear groans. She and Peg went to a courtyard in which the injured had been placed in long rows. At first they could do nothing but comfort their patients, but, within minutes, ambulances and emergency crews from all of the Dutton hospitals arrived; and they took orders from a lean, gray-haired doctor they had never seen before. He didn't waste time on introductions.

"Some of these people are already in shock," he said. "Take blankets and cover them up. Don't try to move them until we can get them to a hospital. If you think whole blood or plasma is called for, come get me. We have a limited supply; I'll have to decide who gets it."

It was her first disaster, and for a moment the sum total of all the suffering which lay before her en masse

70

threatened to overwhelm her. But she was a professional healer, and she forced herself to think of the injured, not as personalities, but as medical cases.

She moved among them, spilling sulpha powder into lacerated flesh, applying tourniquets to bleeders, helping the doctors to put rude splints on fractures that would be set when the patients were removed to hospitals. Stretchers bore what seemed to be an unending number of patients into ambulances and other vehicles; but more were being dug out of the rubble every minute.

Ruth spoke quietly to each patient. "I'm a nurse. Let me help you."

"I want my mother," a little boy cried. "The wind blew my mother away." His left leg had been crushed by a toppling refrigerator. Neither of his parents had been found.

"We'll find your mother," Ruth promised. *And I hope we find her alive,* she added silently.

A gray-haired woman stood looking vacantly at the gaping brickwork where her third-story apartment had been. "Where are my girls?" she said wildly. "Both of my girls were there when I went to work this morning."

A neighbor patted her on the shoulder. "Come, Mrs. Robbins," he said. "I'll take you to check the hospitals."

Gillis had approached, and he pulled the man aside for a moment while the woman walked ahead. "If they're not there," Ed said, "you'd better check the armory. They've turned it into an emergency morgue." The man nodded grimly.

"Ruth," Ed said, "we need you." She nodded and followed him to where a figure lay on the ground. After a while she could see that it was a girl. Dirt and sand had been driven into her flesh by the force of the wind when it had hit her, and she looked as if she wore a gray and black crust. Something about her twisted position caught Ruth's attention.

"Did she fall?" she asked.

"From the third floor," Ed said. "The clotheslines caught her before they snapped."

"Don't touch her," Ruth said. "I'll try to get an ambulance."

When she finally located one, it was from Memorial Hospital. The driver followed her to the girl, carrying a stretcher. "As soon as possible, Miss," he said, "you'd better report back to the hospital. They can't handle all the cases that've been brought in."

"I'll go as soon as I can," she promised. "Do you have any first aid supplies?" He had a small kit, which he gave to her. When the girl had been placed in the ambulance and driven away, Ruth turned to Ed.

"Now I have a job for you," she said.

It wasn't an easy one. One whole courtyard had been filled with injured children. Adults who had been hurt were a bad enough problem, but at least they could be reasoned with. These children knew only that something terrible had happened, that their world had suddenly been ripped into ugly chunks and shreds, that they felt pain—that they wanted their mothers and fathers.

"They have to be treated," Ruth said. "Quiet them if you can. If you can't, hold them by force. It's the only way." She had dealt with children long enough to know that most of them wouldn't be quieted. But Ed was a strong man, and she knew that by force he could hold any youngster long enough for her to administer treatment.

Ed surprised her, however. His deep voice became a caress, an understanding sound from which a child could gain comfort. He talked man-to-man to the boys and like a father to the girls.

"Here, lad," he said to one boy whose body shook so badly with frightened sobs that Ruth couldn't understand him when he told her where he hurt. "Here, you know what this reminds me of? I was with the Second Division the day we broke through Chinese lines at Seoul. You think you're frightened now? You should have seen me that day. I was as scared as anybody can be. But do you know what? At the last minute, I got mad at the Chinese who had made me that scared. I decided I wasn't going to let 'em lick me, and I didn't. Now, we can do the same thing to this big wind that passed over us a few hours ago. It can't lick us unless we let it." The boy's sobbing had stopped. He gasped for breath as he breathed, but his

72

eyes were calmer as he stared at Ed. "Now, son," Ed said. "Where do you hurt?"

"My knee."

Ed started to raise the leg of the dirty slacks, but the boy gasped and turned white. Carefully, the big policeman ripped the fabric straight up the boy's thigh. The knee was swollen and discolored. Ruth set to work with a grateful smile, while Ed stroked his young friend's face with large, square hands that were curiously tender.

Together, the nurse and the detective went down the row of children. Finally, Ruth straightened up from bending over the last one. She sighed.

"Well, that's that," she said. "We've done all we can for them here. Now we'll have to do our best to finish the job when they're hospitalized."

They walked back to the road, too tired for conversation. Ed lit a cigarette and pulled at it deeply. "I'm going back to the hospital," Ruth said.

"I won't be able to drive you," Ed said. "It'll take a long time to go through all this rubble and make sure there's no one left under it. I don't go on duty until tomorrow. They can use me here."

She smiled at him. "I'll get back all right," she said.

There was a taxi standing near the ambulance, and, too tired even to feel surprise, Ruth saw that Gerry Jancowski was standing near it talking to the Civil Defense warden who was directing traffic.

"Listen," Jancowski was saying, "that was my sister's apartment that caved in. Can't you tell me where she is, how she is?"

"I told you before, buddy," the warden explained patiently. "All I know is that the lady was injured. I don't know how bad. They took her away in one of them green ambulances."

"That would be a Memorial Hospital ambulance if it was green," Ruth said. "They must have taken her to Memorial."

"Thanks, lady," Jancowski said. "I'll get right down there." He turned to go, but she stopped him.

"I'm a Memorial nurse," she said. "I've got to get to the hospital. Can I go with you?"

This time Jancowski opened the taxi door for her.

When she walked into the hospital lobby, she gasped. It was packed full of people. Those who could find chairs, sat, and the others leaned against the walls, slumped on the stairs or milled around, talking in a low, frightened murmur. Ruth stopped at the reception desk.

"This is ridiculous," she said. "These people shouldn't be allowed to wait around like this. Emergency or no emergency, they should be told that a hospital must maintain visiting hours in order to function."

The receptionist smiled up at her. "You have it wrong, honey," she said. "They're all waiting to give blood. We appealed to the public for blood donors in a radio broadcast about forty minutes ago. These people showed right up. More are coming all the time."

"Oh," Ruth said. She looked at the donors waiting to give their own strength to help others live. Dutton was showing what it was made of.

In the nurses' lounge she washed hurriedly and changed into a spare uniform somebody threw at her. It was too tight and it threatened to split at the seams, but it was clean and starched.

Peg Collins was running Revere Ward when Ruth got to the third floor. "I wondered what had become of you," Peg said. "I hitched a ride back to the hospital in an ambulance. We've got our hands full tonight. Surgery has been going full blast, and so has Orthopedics. We're going to have to hustle to keep up."

Some of the tiredness dropped off Ruth's shoulders as the need to meet the challenge occurred to her. "We'll hustle," she said grimly.

"Everybody has been working on this thing," Peg said. "All nurses reported in for duty—even the spares."

"They'll be needed before we're through," Ruth said. She started to brush by the other girl, but Peg stopped her for another instant.

"Ruth. . . ." Collins said.

"What is it, Peg?" Ruth asked in concern. She noticed with amazement that Peggy's lips were trembling.

"At a time like this," Peggy said, "aren't you glad that

74

you became a nurse?" She looked half afraid that Ruth would laugh.

Ruth didn't even smile. For a moment they gazed at one another. Then Ruth squeezed her friend on the shoulder. "Very glad," she said.

"Nurse," someone called in the men's section of the ward.

"I'll get it," Ruth said. She hurried to answer the summons.

Chapter Nine

Dutton licked it wounds. The day after the tornado was soft and gentle, and the air was fresh and newborn. Hammers rang and machinery roared in the north end of town as rubble was cleared and rebuilding was started immediately. Some semblance of normality began to return. Business went on as usual.

And Detective-Sergeant Edward Alan Gillis was summoned to Boston to see the Commissioner of Public Safety, commanding officer of the Massachusetts State Police.

Ed was nervous. He had seen the Commissioner only once before, when he had graduated from the training academy at Framingham and the Commissioner had made the commencement speech. Now as he sat in the top man's anteroom, his nerves were on edge.

The lieutenant who functioned as aide, all gleaming puttees and wrinkle-less uniform, nodded at him.

"He'll see you now," he said curtly.

The Commissioner was signing letters when Ed came in. He looked at Gillis, nodded briefly, and went on signing.

"Sit down," he said. Gillis sat. The Commissioner signed the last letter and the middle-aged woman who had waited by his desk took the pile of correspondence from him and walked briskly from the room.

"Know why I called you in?" the Commissioner asked.

He doesn't waste time in chit-chat, Ed thought. "No, sir," he said.

"I wanted to ask you if you think you should be taken off the Dutton case," he said.

Ed met his level gaze steadily, but he said nothing.

"Well?" said the Commissioner. "Should you be?"

"I don't see why," Ed said. "I don't think anyone else could do anything I haven't done, or do better what I have done and am doing."

"Hmmmph," the Commissioner said. It was just a noise. Gillis didn't know whether it meant approval, disapproval, or disbelief. "Do you want some help?" the Commissioner said. "Want to split the assignment with someone?"

"That's up to you," Gillis said. "Sooner or later something will break on the case. When it does, I think I can handle it. If you want to replace me, or send somebody out with me, that's up to you."

The Commissioner continued to stare at him. "You think we have to wait it out, wait for the attacker to make a slip, is that it?"

"I don't see anything else we can do," Ed said. "I've had the boys at the Dutton barracks pull in every crackpot and psycho for fifty miles around. They all check clean. This guy is a new one, somebody we don't know about. I'm sure of it. We'll just have to wait it out."

The Commissioner turned away. "It so happens I agree with you, Sergeant," he said. He pushed a little button on the side of his desk and the gray-haired woman came trotting briskly back into the room. "Go back and wait it out, Sergeant," the Commissioner said.

"Yes, sir," Ed said. The Commissioner was already dictating to his secretary when Gillis closed the door behind him and walked past the stiff-looking lieutenant and on out into the Boston street.

In a drugstore across from the Common, he slipped into a phone booth and dialed. It rang four times, and he was getting ready to replace the receiver when the faded old male voice answered.

"Hello?"

"Hello, Uncle Terence?"

"Is it Edward?"

"It's Edward, Uncle Terence. How are you doin'?"

"I'm doin' well enough to lay you out with one fist tied to the bedpost. When are we goin' to see you? Or are you too busy arrestin' every good man in the whole state?"

"I am today. But I'll be seeing you soon. There's a girl I want you to meet."

There was a short silence. "Are you sure that you want her to meet me?"

"I'm very sure, Terence."

"Then bring her out. I'll have to pick up all the beer cans and throw them away."

Ed laughed. "You do that, you old guzzler, before I run you in."

"When will you be out?"

"I don't know," Ed said. "She's a nurse. I'll have to see when she can get away from the hospital."

"Well, give me ten minutes' warning, so I can sweep the dust under the rug. It'll be good to see you, boy."

"It'll be good to see you, too, Terence."

He realized with faint surprise, as he left the booth and headed back to his car, that it *would* be good to see his uncle, at that.

As a token of appreciation, Memorial Hospital had rewarded the nurses who had worked through the tornado emergency with extra time off, and Ruth found herself with the week end free. When Ed asked her to Boston on Saturday to meet his uncle, she agreed without hesitation. "I'd like that," she told him.

Now, as they drove along through the green New England countryside, he spoke to her about Terence and the things he stood for in Ed's eyes.

"I want you to meet Terence," he said. "I want you to take a good look at the South Side, too. That's where I come from. It was home to me when I was a kid."

"What's it like?" she asked.

"Poor," he said. "Poor, and tough. Everybody who comes from there brags about being a Southy. It's a badge. It means that you learned at a tender age how to use your fists."

"You've never spoken about your parents. They're not alive, are they?" Ruth asked.

"Terence is all I've got," he said. "My mother died in childbirth when I was born. My father died while I was in Korea."

"Was he like you?" Ruth asked.

"He was a crook," Gillis said in a calm, flat voice. She stared at him. "He was a small-timer, the tail end of a big syndicate. They never trusted him with anything important, just illegal errands. He was their errand boy until the day he died."

"Is he why you became a policeman?" she asked.

He nodded. "I reached a point," he said, "when I had to go one way or the other. I was seventeen. I had a job pumping gas in a station on Commonwealth Avenue. One day the old man was sick, and the syndicate had a package to be driven from Boston to Springfield. I suppose it was money—a payoff of some kind. They asked me to take his place.

"I told them no. The old man got up out of bed and drove with a fever of 102. Two hundred miles to deliver a payoff, with a fever of 102. When he came home that night, he threw me out of his flat. Terence took me in."

"How did you become a state trooper?" she asked.

"I was looking for a way out of the South Side. I started going to Boston University night classes. In the back of my mind was the thought of studying law, but I guess I got tired of pumping gas all day and studying all night. When I turned twenty-one I took the state police exam, and I've been a cop ever since."

"We're just a couple of orphans," Ruth said lightly. She smiled at him. "At least you've got Terence."

"I'll share him with you," he said.

A half-hour later Ed pulled the car up in front of a dingy tenement building on a dingy street. He led the way through a littered alleyway to the entrance, and then up

78

four flights of worn stairs, past smells of cabbage and age and stale air.

Terence met them at the top of the stairs. He was small. She had expected a large man like Ed, but he was little and thin, with a shock of white hair, a red face, and blue eyes. He was in his shirt-sleeves and he smoked a corncob pipe.

"Come in, come in," he said. His place was as clean as only a fussy bachelor's apartment can be. The furniture was old and worn, but Ruth could tell at a glance that Terence worried about comfort more than he did about show. She counted four tobacco cans in the little living room. Terence saw her looking at them, and he grinned.

"I keep 'em scattered like that," he said, "so that whenever I feel like a smoke I don't have to go far for my tobacco."

The three settled down to talk. Terence, it turned out, was a bridge-tender.

"Exactly what does a bridge-tender do?" Ruth asked.

"My bridge is over a canal connecting the river with the bay," he said. "It's a low bridge. Whenever a tug or some other vessel comes along, I stop traffic, pull my levers, and the bridge opens up on hinges to let the boat go through."

"I've seen those," Ruth said in delight. "What a fine job!"

"I used to go down to the bridge and wait for a boat to come, so Uncle Terence could raise the span," Ed said. "I bragged about him to all the kids in the neighborhood. Once I even got up a tour; I charged pennies and took a whole gang of kids down with me to see the sight. We waited all afternoon, but not a boat came by. I had to give the kids their pennies back."

"Tell me about Ed when he was a little boy," Ruth said to Terence.

"I have some pictures, if you'd care to see them," he said.

Ed objected strenuously, but soon the old man and the girl were going through the album, expressing their opinions freely while he pretended not to listen.

The afternoon passed quickly.

"Does McSweeney's on the corner still make a specialty of corned beef and cabbage?" Ed asked.

"That they do," Terence said. "Do you like the combination, girl?"

"That I do," Ruth replied, trying to get just the touch of brogue that flavored Terence's speech into her own words.

Ed went down for three orders, and they dined regally on corned beef prepared the way it was meant to be.

Ruth insisted on doing the dishes alone, and the two men sat and smoked while she got them out of the way. Terence sighed in satisfaction.

"I'd like to have guests like this every night," he said.

There was a battered upright in the parlor, and after the dishes were done Terence sat on the chipped black stool and played all the old Irish songs; and the three of them sang of Molly Malone and her wheelbarrow, of the potato famine, and of the plight of Patrick on the railroad.

It was nine o'clock when Terence rose with a sigh and reluctantly dropped the lid over the piano keys.

"I'm afraid I'll have to chase you," he said. "I'm tendin' my bridge tonight, and I'd best be getting down there."

Ruth said good-by with regret.

"I've had a good time," she said.

"Come again," he told her as he took her hand. "Come down to the bridge and I'll raise it just for you."

They drove slowly through the city. "I like him," Ruth told Ed. "I'll gladly accept a half interest in Terence Gillis."

He smiled. They were passing the Public Gardens. "Want to ride the swan boats?" he asked.

"I don't know what they are, but they sound like fun. Let's," she said.

A few minutes later they were at the pond and boarding the big white boat with the large swan figurehead. They sat on a deck bench while the crew cast off, and the boat drifted serenely over the surface of the pond. Other boats glided by them, looking in the darkness like great replicas of their swan namesakes. The sounds of the traffic sifted to them through the night as if from a far-off land.

Ed took her hand in his. "Just a couple of orphans," he said.

"A couple of innocent babes alone in the big, cold world," she said.

"You're not alone."

She felt the pressure of his hand as it tightened over her own. "I know," she said.

On the pond the boats moved slowly, like huge white swans.

Chapter Ten

The Autumn Festival was a combination variety show and formal ball at the country club. It was Memorial Hospital's big social event of the year, a time for godlike surgeons to relax and act human toward the nurses who ordinarily trembled at their slightest frown, a time to forget about sickness and pain, a short respite from duty in which to relearn that the world is a place full of laughter and hot jazz music.

When the first posters went up on the bulletin boards, announcing the festival, Allie MacKenzie asked Ruth if he could take her to it. His name was listed as festival chairman—a preview, she told herself, of the social prominence his mother wanted for him.

"Won't you be too busy for a date?" she asked.

"I would for most dates," he said. Both of them grinned. "Actually," he said, "my duties will keep me busy before the festival, not during it. And as long as I'm going to be tied up all the time, why don't you get yourself a job on one of the committees? That way I won't have to worry about the long arm of the law reaching out and grabbing you while my back is turned."

"You fool," she said, "this is exactly what I've been waiting for. The height of my social season begins this

Thursday evening, and when word circulates that I'm not dated up, I expect the phone at Mrs. Hanscom's to ring and ring."

But when she left him and walked to Revere, she felt an impatient little tingle—the old sensation of wanting to be in on everything before it happened—that had kept her so busy in school.

"Let's volunteer for festival jobs," she said to Collins.

Peggy looked up from her task of making up medications for the cart. She let a pained look settle on her good-natured Irish face.

"Sure," she said. "Let's do that. With all our spare time. In between trips to Newport and cruises on our yacht. Listen, Mason, it may be news to you, but I'm a nurse. When I finish nursing Revere Ward, my feet hurt."

On the following afternoon, however, both girls happened to be in the hospital early, having arranged to meet for dinner in the staff cafeteria. Collins had just been asked to the festival by Dr. Rawlings, the new intern, and she was in an unusually gay mood.

"He's directing it," she told Ruth.

"Who's directing what?" Ruth asked blankly.

"Ted. Ted Rawlings. He's directing the variety show. He used to play summer stock when he was pre-med." She grabbed Ruth's arm and stared earnestly into her eyes. "Tell me the truth. Isn't he just terrific?"

"I'm inclined to be rather cautious in my descriptions, you know," Ruth said. "But if you say so. . . ."

"He auditioning the show right now in the auditorium. It's early. Let's go watch," Peggy said. "That way all the wilted, leftover salads from lunch will be used up, and we'll get to the cafeteria in time for the fresh ones."

"Sold," Ruth said.

They strolled to the auditorium, straight into a scene from Tin Pan Alley. Ted Rawlings stood in front of the piano with a cigarette dangling from his mouth and a look of sheer despair on his face. A scattering of spectators sat in the plush seats of the hall, but everyone seemed to have come to watch and not to volunteer his services.

"Look," Dr. Rawlings was saying. "We're all friends here. There's nothing to feel bashful about. Now let's get started, huh?" For a moment an embarrassed silence hung over the group, and then someone in the back of the hall tittered nervously. The sound was infectious, and soon others were laughing outright. It was silly, shamed laughter, aimed more at themselves than at the young doctor standing in front of them trying to play director, but a slow red flush began to show above the top of Ted Rawlins' white collar.

Collins looked miserable. "What'll we do?" she whispered to Ruth.

"What can we do?" Ruth said. "I wish there were some way we could help the poor fella, but . . ."

Suddenly Peggy got to her feet. "Dr. Rawlings," she said.

He saw her for the first time, and he seemed to grow even more miserable with the realization that she had witnessed his embarrassment.

"Dr. Rawlings," Peggy said, "we want to audition." She grabbed her friend by the hand; before Ruth knew what was happening, she was being led down the aisle toward the front of the hall. She felt a cloud of panic settle over her as stage fright numbed her body.

"Wait a minute, Collins," she said. "I can't."

"You've got to," Peggy said, without turning her head. "Anyway, you said just yesterday that you wanted to do something for the festival."

"I wanted to serve on a committee!" Ruth said.

Ted Rawlings looked as if he could have kissed them both. "What'll it be, girls?" he said. "Dance?"

Collins looked at Ruth, and Ruth slowly shook her head.

"We don't dance," Collins said.

"Comic routine?"

Again the questioning look, and once more Ruth shook her head.

"Do you sing?" The doctor's voice was beginning to get a little hoarse with strain.

Peggy's eyes pleaded, so Ruth shrugged. "Everybody sings," she said.

Relief flooded into Ted Rawlings' face. "What'll it be, girls?" he said.

Ruth was beginning to feel light-headed and devil-may-care.

"What do you like?" she said. "We know them all."

"How about 'Daisy, Daisy'?" the doctor suggested. Luckily, it was one of the few songs Ruth remembered from her childhood days.

"Hit it, Professor," she said. Ted Rawlings played a good, loud piano, and the girls did their best. The result wasn't grand opera, but everyone said later that it wasn't bad, either. Ruth had always enjoyed singing, and after the first few bars she relaxed and pretended it was just another songfest at a beach party.

They finished with a fine burst of sound that was applauded enthusiastically by the onlookers. Several people got up and came forward.

"How about an Italian number, Doc?" asked Mike Leofanti, an X-ray technician. "Do you know 'O Sole Mio'?"

"If I don't," Ted Rawlings said, "I'll learn it."

Singly and in small groups, hospital workers who had been too shy to audition until the ice was broken were getting up and walking toward the piano.

"I don't know how we're going to work it, because, to tell you the truth, even with Patti, Maxine and Laverne you wouldn't be the Andrews Sisters. But one thing is sure—as far as this show is concerned, you're in."

"Oh, fine . . ." Ruth said.

Ted Rawlings was a talented showman, and within a few days he had come up with an act for the girls, all trick lighting and gimmickry, designed to draw attention from the fact that their voices left much to be desired.

It was a take-off on the old Ted Lewis routine built around "Me and My Shadow." Dr. Rawlings decked the girls out in a couple of cut-down tuxedos and rubbed burnt cork on Ruth's face so she could be a proper shadow. Then he taught them a simple buck-and-wing step, and they were all ready to perform.

"Be plaintive," he said. "Your get-ups are funny, so they'll draw all the boffs you'll need. Basically, though, it's a sad song when you come right down to it. Don't be afraid to let the audience know that it's a tune about loneliness.

Pretend that you might break down and cry at any moment."

"Who has to pretend?" Collins asked. "We're so scared, it could happen."

Actually, though, both girls were enjoying the experience tremendously.

"I'm going to ask my sister and my brother-in-law to drop in and watch us," Collins said. "The ball will be a closed affair, but I don't think anyone will mind if they come in to see the show."

Ruth had been thinking along the same lines. The next time she saw Allie MacKenzie, she asked him about it.

"I'm going to be your date," she said, "but I was wondering if you'd mind if I invited somebody to drop in and see Peggy and me on the stage?"

Allie grinned, but he didn't succeed in looking very happy. "The gendarme?" he asked.

"Yes," Ruth said. "Ed Gillis."

"Ask him to drop in, by all means," Allie said, "but remember, as soon as curtain comes down and the burnt cork comes off—you're mine, all mine."

"Is that an order, Doctor?"

"That's an order." For a moment it sounded as if he really meant it, and the smile stiffened on her face. Her eyes held his for a long second, then looked away, and she spoke quietly:

"I'd better go find a phone and give Ed a ring, so he won't miss seeing the entertainment attraction of the century."

"If I know that guy," Allie said, "he knew ten minutes ago that you were going to call him, and he's got the tie he'll wear to the show all picked out."

But he grinned as she stuck out her tongue at him.

Chapter Eleven

The night of the festival was cool and moonless, a detail Dr. Alden MacKenzie looked upon with disapproval as he drove homeward from the hospital in his convertible. It had been a particularly bright August, with the moon and stars out almost every night, and he felt that September was letting him down.

"Come out, old Moon," he said to himself as he drove the car up Pool Hill. "I can use all the help I can get tonight."

It had been a rough day, and he was glad to be away from the smell of sickness for a few hours. He parked the car and ran upstairs to grab a quick shower. There was a lot to be done before he could pick up Ruth.

His mother spoke through his closed door while he was toweling.

"Alden," she said, "that orchestra fellow called. He got the extra pieces you asked for."

"Good," he said. He frowned as he pushed a stud through his stiff white shirt-front. Maybe his mother was right about these chairmanships being a social duty, but he was sure going to try to make himself scarce the next time duty came a-knocking at his door. He wondered what Ruth was going to wear.

He put on a plaid cummerbund and then stepped back to admire the sight of himself grinning out of the mirror in evening clothes. Jazzy. Definitely jazzy. Quite a relief from the solid clinical whites he had been wearing day in and day out lately.

On the way downstairs he stopped at his mother's room and stuck in his head to say good night.

"Come here for a moment and let me see you," Elizabeth MacKenzie said. She looked as if she had been napping. Her cheek had little red marks on it where the small chenille bumps of the bedspread had pressed into it. She smiled at him.

"Have a good day at the hospital?" she asked.

"The usual," he said. He was about to rush off when he noticed with a sudden sense of dismay that her lower lip was trembling and her eyes were filling with tears.

"Mother," he said gently. "What's the matter, dear?"

"Nothing, really," she said. "I'm just getting old, that's all."

"What is it?" he asked. "You know that's not so."

"Oh, I can remember when I used to go to these things with your father, and now you go to them and I stay at home and watch you go."

He felt like a guilty little boy. "I should have asked you, I suppose," he said slowly, "but I've been so busy with the arrangements on top of my regular work at the hospital. . . . Why not get dressed and I'll stop by for you in half an hour, huh?"

"You have a date, haven't you, Alden?"

"Yes, Mother, I do," he said. "I'm taking Ruth. But I'm sure she'd be glad to see you."

"You're sure of no such thing," Elizabeth MacKenzie said, "and you know it."

"As a matter of fact," he said, "this is one night when I don't want you or anybody around when I'm with her."

Elizabeth looked up sharply. There were no tears in the blue eyes now. Suddenly they were clear and very wary.

"You're not going to do anything hasty, are you, Son?" she said.

"I'm going to ask her to marry me."

Elizabeth forced herself to check the flow of words that sprang into her mouth. She was a shrewd woman, and she knew her son.

"Are you sure?" she asked.

"I'm sure," he said.

She reached up and kissed his cheek. "Then good luck," she told him. "But don't stay out too late. You have to go to the hospital so early in the morning."

"I won't, Mom," he promised.

She sat in her room and listened to the noise of her son descending the stairs, the slam of the door as he left the house, the clatter of his car's starter and the smooth purr of the Olds motor. She was thinking hard. The phone was within reach of her arm; she lifted the receiver from the cradle and dialed the number of her attorney, a judge who had watched out for her family's interests since the day he had graduated from Harvard Law School with her father-in-law, forty-seven years before.

She was gracious and soft-spoken when he came to the phone, although he had kept her waiting for almost five minutes—which wasn't common practice for anyone dealing with Mrs. MacKenzie. However, she accepted the delay as another facet of a bad day.

"Judge," she said, when he finally spoke into the phone, "this is Elizabeth. I have a job for you. Find out whatever you can about a Memorial nurse named Ruth Mason. I want a complete history."

When she had hung up she sat there in the falling darkness, fingering the fading marks of the chenille bumps on her cheek, and telling herself that engagements had been broken many, many times before.

Chapter Twelve

It started out like every other hospital function he had ever been to—quiet, orderly, and dull. He was busy acting the part of the efficient chairman, and it made him glum to see luckier men arriving with their dates on their arms. He and Ruth had agreed that it would be a lot more practical if she came to the country club herself, since she would have to get into her costume and makeup for the show, and he would be so busy running things.

He was standing in the reception line when Ed Gillis

sauntered in, looking comfortably out of place, a gray-suit island surrounded by a sea of tuxedos.

"Hello, Gendarme," Allie said. "I can't imagine what brings you here."

"You have very little imagination," Gillis grinned. "Does it matter where I sit?"

"I have two reserved. You might as well sit with me."

"I accept your invitation. Is there time for me to buy you a drink?"

Allie suddenly felt very tired of shaking hands and saying, "So glad you could come." Nobody, he knew, would miss him if he left his place at the door.

"We'll make time," he said.

They had tall, cool gin-and-tonics at the bar, lingering over them in companionable silence. When they were finished, Allie motioned to the bartender.

"My turn," he told Ed.

The show was just about to start when they hustled to their seats. Ruth and Peg were the fourth act to go on, and they had to suffer through three jugglers who kept dropping their Indian clubs. "They're all surgeons," Allie told Ed, "and I hope they never drop that many scalpels." Mike Leofanti's *"O Sole Mio,"* and a teeter-toed ballet by Dr. Anderson's eleven-year-old daughter, followed.

Finally, however, the girls were on. If they were nervous, they didn't show it. They mugged, waved their tall silk hats and gave out with just the proper amounts of humor and pathos.

When their stint was over they drew more applause than had any of the preceding acts. Allie and Ed pounded their palms until they stung, and when they found that they were clapping alone as the hall finally fell silent, they stopped and grinned at one another.

"She did all right, didn't she?" Ed said.

"She did just fine."

They suffered through the rest of the show together, and when the final curtain came down Allie went backstage to claim his date. Ruth was waiting for him, and, when he saw her, his breath caught in his throat.

"You're lovely," he told her. She wore a white gown that accented the deep tan of her skin; and her blonde hair, usually gathered into a bun beneath her cap, hung in unconfined ringlets on her shoulders.

The club was a mass of balloons and paper streamers. The band was playing, and the show had served to loosen people up so that everyone seemed to be in a party mood.

He took her by the hand and led her onto the dance floor. He slipped on a piece of paper streamer, and, as he caught himself from falling, he laughed. He must have laughed too loudly, because Ruth had a strange look on her face as she stared at him.

"Have you been drinking?" she asked quietly.

"Just one or two," he said, "while I was waiting for you."

They circled the floor once, and then Dr. Anderson cut in. Allie waited around for a few minutes and, just as he was getting ready to cut back in, he saw Ed Gillis walk onto the floor and tap Dr. Anderson's shoulder. He was watching the detective dance by him with his girl when Dr. Anderson walked over to him.

"Stop looking so unhappy, Alden," the older man said. "It's going to be a long evening. Come on, I'll buy you a drink."

He knew that it wouldn't please Ruth if he had more alcohol, but Dr. Anderson was his superior, after all, he told himself. He had a drink with Anderson and he had just ordered another when Ruth came into the bar and glanced at him in a way that almost sobered him up on the spot.

"Why look at me like that?" he asked her. His hand went into the pocket of his tuxedo jacket, and his fingers closed around the small square box containing the ring he had bought that morning.

"You're my escort, are you not?"

"Sure," he said. "Want something to drink?"

"How can you act like this?" she whispered. He had never seen her angry before, and he noted with surprise that her green eyes looked almost black.

He led her back onto the floor, stopping first to whisper a request to the orchestra leader. The song was "Me and My Shadow," and they started to play it at once.

Ruth tried to stay angry, but then she grinned in spite of herself, and they both laughed.

They danced in silence, twice around the floor, and it was very nice. She even sang a little of the song.

It felt good, not looking at her, the sweet smell of her perfumed hair, listening to her high, thin little voice as he held her in his arms while they danced.

But the dance ended and they drifted toward the bar. "Let me buy you a drink," he said. "A *soft* drink," he added hastily, and they laughed again.

She wanted cider. "With lots of ice," she told the bartender. But the man shook his head.

"Sorry, Miss," he said. "We don't have it. Not enough people ask for it for us to stock it at affairs like this. How about punch? Or a carbonated drink?"

"Nope," Ruth said. "Thanks anyway."

"You're spoiled," Allie told her. She smiled and opened her mouth to say something, but then Ted Rawlings was there.

"Stag line claimed my girl," Rawlings said. "Can I borrow yours?"

Allie watched them walk onto the floor. They hadn't taken three steps before Ed Gillis tapped Rawlings on the shoulder. Allie watched Gillis and Ruth dance into the crowd.

"The place is full of state cops," he told the bartender. He had another drink, and when the thought came to him it seemed like the most logical idea in the world.

She wanted cider. The bar didn't stock cider. But he knew where there was cider. Lots of cider. So he'd go get her some.

He wasn't very drunk, he told himself. He was proud of the way he wove the Olds out of the crowded club parking lot without so much as touching another car. The motor stalled a couple of times, though.

"Oh, you're high, all right, MacKenzie," he said aloud, and he chuckled.

He had complete control of his senses, however, he thought. He even remembered to shut off his lights be-

91

fore starting the car each time the motor stalled, because he had heard somewhere that starting a car with the beams on caused a big drain on the battery. But he must have stalled again on the orchard road and forgotten to put his lights back on again after he started the car, because he drove along through the dark night with no illumination ahead, lazily traveling the familiar route with the top of the convertible down and the black air pouring softly around him, fluttering his tie and pushing warm fingers of wind through his hair.

He heard the thump off the right fender, but it never occurred to him that he should stop. "Must be a rabbit," he said aloud. "Poor little rabbit. Ain't never gonna run no more." The words pleased him as he sang them out into the night to the tune of "Me and My Shadow."

"Pooo-ore li'l ole ra-ab-bit, ain' nev' gone run no moooo. . . ."

Pretty big bump for a rabbit, he thought then. Maybe a fox. He hoped that it hadn't been a dog. *Stupid farmers,* he thought; *they let their dogs run around on the loose, so it might have been a dog at that.*

He pulled up by the orchard packing-shed and leaned on his horn, splitting the quiet with a long, wailing note. He chuckled as he saw Stash's flashlight bobbing down the loading platform toward him. The old man turned the flash on him.

"Who there?" he quavered. "What you want?"

Allie blinked and closed his eyes.

"Shut that thing off," he said. "It's me, Allie Mac-Kenzie. Sell me some cider, will you, Stash?"

Stash chuckled in delight when he saw who it was. Anything Allie did was always all right with him. From force of habit, however, he lectured him: "Whatsa matter with you, Allie, you crazy or somethin'? You come down here with no lights on, like to kill yourself, an' you make a lotta noise. My woman's asleep. You know what time it is?"

"Heck, Stash," Allie said, "I know that road so well I can drive it in my sleep, never mind without lights. Come on, be a good guy. The cider's for Ruth."

"Ha! For you I wouldn't, but for the pretty nurse I

92

will." Stash shuffled off into one of the sheds and came out with a jug, which he passed over to Allie. He ignored the bill Allie held out to him. "Come back when you're not drunk, young doctor," he said, playfully roughing up Allie's head with a calloused palm.

He stood on his platform and watched the car shoot off down the road until it was swallowed by the blackness.

"And put on your lights!" he roared. Then he chuckled, standing on the dark platform and remembering other days when he had done foolish and reckless things to impress his Bronislawa.

The noise behind him was no more than a creaking board, but habit made him turn to see what it was. The beam of his flashlight gleamed on the knife blade as it came down. He tried to evade it, but he was old and slow. The blade struck again and again. With his last strength, Stash held the beam so it shone in his assailant's face.

"You!" he said.

The only answer was the blade that rose and fell until it was unnecessary for it to strike any more.

Allie drove for several minutes until he remembered that Stash had yelled something to him as he had pulled away from the shed. What was it? His thinking processes were fuzzy, all full of cotton batting. *Oh, yeah,* he told himself, *the lights.* When he switched them on, only the left one worked, and he stopped the car and went around to the front to see what was wrong. The lamp was shattered. The other headlight showed brown spots all over the black fender.

And then he saw the rag.

It was caught in the crack between the body and the hood, a piece of dirty white cloth, looking as if it had been ripped from a man's undershirt. He picked it up and stood there with it in his hand, trying to comprehend what it meant.

He got back into the car slowly, using the spotlight, playing the beam up and down the side of the road.

He saw the boy almost right away.

The kid was small, a thin Negro boy in sneakers and blue jeans, with half his tee-shirt gone from his back. He was lying face down, and in the bad light he looked like an oversized rag doll that someone had tired of playing with. He started to turn the boy over.

"Be alive. Be alive," someone was saying, and he realized that he was talking out loud. There was a .22 rifle near the kid. Its stock was broken, and the sight of the splintered wood made him sad.

He felt cold sober.

With hands experience had made as sensitive as a woman's, he checked the boy's body. The clavicle was fractured, and so was the left hip. But the patient was breathing.

He was beginning to feel exultant when he noticed the thin trickle of blood that had welled from the boy's mouth. That wasn't so good, he told himself. That was bad. It could mean nothing at all or it could mean that the kid was dying. There was no way to check for internal injuries.

Gently, tenderly, all doctor, he picked up the unconscious boy and placed him on the back seat. He took off his tuxedo jacket and covered his patient with it. Then he got into the front seat, started the car, and traveled as fast as he could without jarring the boy—straight for Memorial Hospital.

It was two hours later when he got home. He stood before the mirror in his room, staring at the sight he made in the mirror—jacketless, his white evening shirt bloodstained, his hair wild and uncombed.

His mother knocked at the door, then opened it. "Can I get you a cup of tea, dear?" she asked. When she saw him she grew pale, but she listened in silence.

"Don't do anything until I've called the judge," she said finally.

"We have time for that, Mother," he said. "I've got to report the accident. I should have done it hours ago."

He was trembling with fatigue and shock, so she dialed the club for him and asked for Ed Gillis. When Ed didn't respond to the paging there, Allie took the phone himself and called the State Police barracks.

They had to send upstairs for him, but finally Gillis came to the phone.

"Hello, Sergeant?" Allie said. "This is Dr. MacKenzie. Sergeant, I ran over a kid. On the orchard road. I don't know. Sergeant, I think—he's hurt pretty bad."

Chapter Thirteen

Ruth felt as if she were caught in the throes of a bad dream when she reported for work the next evening. The memory of the night before filled her with a sad, hopeless fury. When, she asked herself, was she going to learn that men could disappoint and hurt?

She had known that Allie MacKenzie was weak and spoiled, but she had felt that deep down he was a man who could be depended on, and he had failed her.

Collins didn't look at her when she walked into the nurses' station.

"Hi, Peg," Ruth said. "Good time last night?"

"Fine," Collins said. "Ruth—I wish you'd stayed with us instead of taking a cab home."

"I had a headache anyhow," Ruth said. She turned misery-filled eyes toward the other girl. "Peg, where could he have gone?"

"Haven't you heard?" Peg asked quietly. "Honey, I'm afraid he's in jail."

Ruth felt the blood rushing from her extremities, leaving her wobbly in the knees, and she sank into a chair by the writing table.

"What for?" she asked.

"There's a kid in 327," Collins said quietly. "Hit by a car. All I know is that Allie brought him in here last night and said he had hit him. Then this morning, when he didn't show up for duty, somebody here called up and found out that he was in jail. The kid's been bleeding from the mouth, and his chart says there's evidence of internal injuries."

Ruth reached for the phone and dialed the number of the State Police barracks, going through the routine of asking for Ed automatically, waiting for his voice in a vacuum of numb despair.

"Hello?" He sounded brusque and tough. His voice belonged to a man accustomed to listening to hysterical women.

"Ed," she said, "it's Ruth. Is it true about Allie?"

"All I know," he said, his voice suddenly gentle, "is that he's been booked and we're holding him. Whatever else there is to the story will have to be decided by judge and jury."

"But it's wrong," she protested wildly. "He may have had too much to drink, he may have hurt this boy badly —but he's not a criminal, to be thrown into jail. Can't you talk to the officer who arrested him, Ed? After all, he took the boy to the hospital. It wasn't hit-and-run, or anything like that. . . ."

"I brought him in, Ruth," Ed said, so softly that she had to strain to hear him.

"You?" she said.

"It's nothing so simple as hit-and-run," he said.

"Then what are you holding him for?" she asked.

The words sounded short and ugly, like the slap of a palm across the face: "Suspicion of murder."

There was a long pause. "You're joking," she said.

"It's nothing I'd joke about," Ed said. "MacKenzie told me that the last person who saw him was Stash Kwiatkowski. He had gone to Stash's to get you some cider. When I went to the apple farm to check out his story I found Stash dead. He had been stabbed, just like all the others."

"Oh, no," she whispered. As a nurse she was used to death, but in the few times she had seen him she had grown very fond of the gnarled old apple-grower, and now she began to cry silently.

96

"Allie was his friend," she said into the phone. "You know that Allie couldn't have done a thing like that."

"I'm a cop," he said. "In my business we have to leave personalities out of our work." He sounded stubborn, but he sounded very unhappy as well.

"The kid MacKenzie hit:" he said, "do you know who it was?"

"No," she said dully.

"It was Seth," he said. "You remember. The Wreck's boy. He asked me whether I thought the kid was old enough to own a .22 and I told him sure. If I had minded my own business the kid wouldn't have been there in the woods last night. He wouldn't have been on the orchard road. He wouldn't have been hit by that car. . . ."

"Stop it!" Ruth said sharply. "It wasn't your fault, and you know it. Any more than those murders were Allie's fault. All you have to do is use a little common sense——"

"Yeah," he cut in. His voice was cold and distant, suddenly, as if it belonged to someone she knew not at all. "Look, I'm busy here. I'll call you tonight before I leave, okay?"

She wondered what was keeping him busy. Was he going to hang up the phone and go directly from talking to her to questioning Allie?

"Don't go out of your way to call," she said, "if you find that you're very busy tonight." The coldness in her voice matched his own.

"Good-by," he said.

"Good-by."

She returned the receiver to the cradle slowly. Just before she set it down she heard a loud click, as if he had slammed his phone heavily as he rang off. The sound was clear and final.

It seemed to signify, to her, the end of something very precious.

She had never known The Wreck's last name until she saw it on the hospital chart at the foot of his son's bed. Jones. Seth Jones. The boy lay quietly, his face gray in the shaded light.

97

Ruth stayed in the background, not daring to intrude upon the group which stood by the bedside. Dr. Anderson moved his hand lightly over the patient's abdomen, his sensitive fingertips gently pressing and probing.

Suddenly Seth Jones, unconscious and under sedation, screamed.

Dr. Anderson looked at the boy's face. "What do you think, Doctor?" he said to Ted Rawlings.

Ted studied his patient. He had profited from experience and he had learned not to make hasty judgments. "There are several possibilities, Doctor," he said slowly. "I would have to investigate more fully, but I think that this patient is suffering from a ruptured spleen. There has been a little bleeding from the mouth, but as yet there has been no hemorrhaging, no indication of splenorrhagia. If further examination bears out this diagnosis, I should think that removal of the spleen would result in a favorable prognosis."

Dr. Anderson continued to watch Seth. "Tell me what you know about the spleen, Doctor," he said.

A faint worry-line creased Ted's forehead. Without being bombastic about it, he had nevertheless committed himself, and he knew Dr. Anderson well enough to be apprehensive. "It's a ductless, gland-like organ," he said carefully. "Oval in shape, vascular, about 200 grams in weight, on the average."

"Where is it located?" Dr. Anderson asked.

Ted licked his lips. "Below the diaphragm," he said. He spoke very slowly, and Ruth knew that in his mind's eye he was seeing the anatomy chart with its familiar multi-colored maze of organs. "In the upper abdominal quarter to the left of the cardiac end of the stomach."

Dr. Anderson reached out once more and touched the boy's abdomen with his fingertips. "Below the diaphragm," he repeated. "Upper abdominal quarter . . . left of cardiac end of stomach." When he reached the place described he probed lightly once more, and again Seth screamed, a shrill cry of pain that filled the room.

"Possible perisplenitis," Dr. Anderson said. "If the liver is affected, prognosis will be very bad." He looked up. "I would say that your diagnosis is probably correct.

Have the usual tests made and order him prepared for surgery. We'll remove the spleen."

"Who'll do the operation?" Ted asked.

"Dr. Gottlieb. I'll assist. You'd better come along and observe, if you can get away."

Ted nodded. He turned. "Nurse," he said, "this patient is to be prepared for surgery." But Ruth had already started for the nurses' station, listing in her mind, as she walked, the steps she would have to take to prepare Seth Jones for his operation.

She saw Dr. Anderson once more that night, just before he went in to scrub.

"Doctor," she said hesitantly. He looked at her sharply, his eyes seeing only the white uniform; and then he recognized her, and his face relaxed kindly.

"Hello, Mason," he said. "Busy night, eh?"

"Doctor." she said again, "just what are the patient's chances?"

"This is a special case, isn't it, Mason?" he asked.

She nodded wordlessly.

"We all think that Allie MacKenzie is a fine boy and a promising doctor," he said. "The other mess he's in is ridiculous, and I'm sure time will solve that. As for this one—we'll do our best to see that everything modern medicine knows will be used to help this patient pull through." Then he added softly, "In a case like this, no one can predict."

Now, as she sat in the silent nurses' station and waited, her nerves rebelled.

"I've got to do something," she told Collins.

"What can you do?" asked Peg. "All you can do is wait."

"At least I can watch," Ruth said. "Things are quiet here now. If you get busy, I'll be in the amphitheater."

"Ruth," Peggy said. "Do you think it's wise? Perhaps you should stay here. . . ."

But she shook her head wordlessly and hurried toward the elevator. The operating room was in the basement, and the amphitheater was on the ground floor. When nurses and interns observed operations as part of their classroom work, it was brightly lighted; but now, as she pushed open the swinging doors, the place was dark. She walked down to the front row of seats and sat down, pressing her forehead gratefully against the cool plate glass as she watched the scene below.

Seth Jones had just been transferred from the cart onto the operating table, and Dr. Caldwell, the anesthetist, was placing the cone over his face. A group came through the door in single file, like a pack of children dressed up in sheets at Halloween, and Ruth recognized Ted Rawlings' stocky figure in whites and Dr. Anderson's spare frame draped in surgical green. She couldn't tell who the nurses were behind their masks. Dr. Gottlieb came last, hurrying as usual, and the others made way for him as he approached the table.

Ruth watched while Dr. Anderson and Dr. Gottlieb conferred. Dr. Anderson drew the incision line on Seth's exposed abdomen; Dr. Gottlieb asked a question, and then nodded. He consulted extensively with the anesthetist, and Ruth, from her own operating room experience, knew why: An anesthetist can mean the success or failure of an operation. An overdose of anesthetic can kill, and an insufficient amount can allow pain to come roaring in to produce shock. The anesthetist must manipulate his knobs and nozzles as skillfully and watchfully as the pilot of a four-engined bomber.

Finally, however, all of the careful preparatory work that precedes actual surgery had been completed. Ruth watched with the fascination that never failed to grip her during moments such as this one, as Dr. Gottlieb held out his palm and the surgical nurse slapped a scalpel into it.

She thought of how surgeons' hands, like concert pianists' hands, are traditionally supposed to be long-fingered and beautiful. And then she thought of how Dr. Gottlieb's hands, now encased in thin rubber gloves, looked when they were gloveless. They had short, stubby fingers, red and tender-looking from much scrubbing with strong soap and very hot water. They were covered with short, thick, black hairs. They looked more like the hands of a bricklayer than those of a surgeon.

And yet she had heard it said that with them he had performed miracles.

Perform one now, she urged him silently.

The scalpel made a swift, clean line across the boy's abdomen, and Ruth watched while the blood that welled up was sponged away, and clamps were applied to the incision.

"Miss Mason?"

She started. It was the elevator operator, standing in the doorway, silhouetted against the bright yellow light outside.

"Miss Mason," he said, "are you in there?"

She cleared her throat. "What is it?" she asked.

"Miss Mason, Miss Collins said for me to tell you that she's sorry, but she needs your help. She says that the roof's fallen in, and she can't handle the ward by herself."

Ruth smiled. She had suspected that Peg would send for her, just to get her away from the operation. But she couldn't refuse to come, because she had no way of knowing whether or not Peggy was pretending.

"I'll come with you now," she said softly. She was surprised, when she stood up, to discover that her knees were trembling. She didn't look down at the group of Halloween ghosts clustered around the table below, their heads bent over their tasks with such concentration that for them the whole world consisted of one small, tiled room containing a patient fighting for his life.

When she returned to the ward she found that, just as she had suspected, things were quiet and there had been no real need for Collins to have summoned her. But she knew that Peg had done the right thing, so she made no issue of the matter. For twenty minutes she checked patients and fussed with charts, and then once again her shrieking nerves betrayed her.

"I'm going back," she told Peg. "Call me again only if you need me." This time Collins didn't even protest.

Ruth saw that it was all over when she entered the amphitheater. Dr. Gottlieb was just dropping a reddish-purple organ from surgical tongs into a laboratory jar, and Ruth knew that the spleen was being sent to the lab for testing and examination that might aid in the next

101

case of this nature to come along. Dr. Anderson was showing Ted Rawlings a special method of applying sutures, and Ruth hurried out of the amphitheater and down the stairs.

She was waiting for the chief surgeon when he came out of surgery.

"Dr. Gottlieb," she said, "I'm a friend of Dr. MacKenzie, whose car it was that hit the patient. Will he— did the operation go as well as you expected?"

He removed the mask with a tired yank; when he spoke his voice was full of controlled anger, not at her, but at a world which demanded that he give it twenty-six hours out of every twenty-four-hour day.

"Child," he said, "I never expect anything when I do an operation that requires me to cut open a human being and take out something that God put in. The splenectomy itself isn't anything much to worry about any more. It used to be a big deal years ago, but nowadays I take out maybe half a dozen a week. What we have to worry about is injury to other organs, notably the liver. I did an examination during the operation, and I couldn't see anything wrong, but of course that doesn't mean a thing. We'll just have to wait and see."

"I'm his ward nurse," she said. "Is there anything special I can do for him?"

He fixed her with an unsmiling stare. "If you've ever learned how to pray," he said, "I don't see how it could possibly hurt the boy's chances." Then he turned and disappeared into the dressing room next door.

She walked up the stairs, feeling empty and helpless. On impulse, as she passed the amphitheater door, she turned and walked inside. She sat down and closed her eyes.

"Please, God," she said aloud. Then, as the words came with a rush, her whispering was the only sound in the empty amphitheater, which was dark and quiet, like a deserted church.

Chapter Fourteen

It was Collins who started the next day cheerfully for Ruth. She was awakened by the sound of Mrs. Hanscom's voice, calling her to the phone. When she answered it sleepily, Peggy's voice shouted into her ear.

"I've got to see you!"

Ruth looked at her bedside clock. "Are you mad, Peg?" she asked. "We both worked until seven this morning, remember? It's only eleven-thirty."

"I've got to see you," Peggy insisted. "I'm at the hospital. Get dressed and hurry on down here."

Ruth felt a momentary pang of alarm. "Is anything wrong?" she asked.

Peggy giggled. "Gosh, no," she said. "Everything's just right. Meet me in the cafeteria."

Baffled, Ruth hung up and swung out of bed, yawning sleepily. "This had better not be her idea of a joke," she mumbled to herself as she groped for her toothbrush.

Half an hour later she walked into the hospital lobby. On her way to the cafeteria she stopped at the information desk, and used the phone to call Revere Ward.

Thomkins, the seven-to-three nurse, answered. "How's Seth Jones doing?" Ruth asked anxiously.

"He's had a fine morning," Thomkins said. "For the first time he seemed actually to sleep instead of just being unconscious, you know what I mean?"

Ruth knew. She had seen it happen many times in cases where the patient had taken a sudden turn for the better.

"Thank goodness," she breathed. But she had also seen enough relapses not to be too jubilant.

"I'll check with you later," she told Thomkins.

She was suppressing a yawn as she walked into the hospital cafeteria. Peggy was at the table in the rear, which she and Ruth always took when it was empty, and with her was Ted Rawlings. Both were grinning like Cheshire cats, Ruth thought.

"How *are* you?" Peggy held out her left hand, which Ruth took somewhat grumpily.

"This is all pretty silly, that's all I can say," she said. "First of all you haul me out of bed, and now you grab my hand just as if we don't see each other thirty times a day—"

Her fingers pressed into something hard and sharp, and she lifted Peg's hand so that she could see the ring. As a diamond it wasn't very impressive, but it was undoubtedly an engagement ring.

She looked into the two pairs of shining eyes, and her own filled. "Oh, I'm so happy for you!" Suddenly both she and Peggy were crying, while Ted squirmed in his chair and eyed people at neighboring tables to see if they were staring.

"When are you going to get married?" she asked.

"Well," Peggy smiled as she dabbed at her eyes with her handkerchief, "frankly, you're discussing the subject of our first quarrel. He doesn't want to marry me."

Ruth turned on Ted. "Are you just toying with this poor girl's affections?" she said.

"It's like the song says," Ted admitted, " 'I can't afford a carriage.' To be honest, I can't afford any kind of marriage right now. I still have more than half my internship to complete, then a year or two of residency here or at some other hospital. . . . Heck, I don't know when we'll be able to get married."

"Methinks," Ruth said, "that the doctor is a chump."

"Huh?" Ted said. He was a little startled.

Ruth grinned. "Do you think this girl is doing you a favor by marrying you? She's been slightly insane ever since you first swung your stethoscope into Revere Ward."

"Wonderful," he said. "But what's your point?"

"She's a nurse. And despite all her grumbling when she flops into a chair after a really tough tour of duty, she loves being a nurse." She turned to Peg. "Right?"

"Right," Peg said hopefully.

"Well, why can't you two get married, then?" Ruth asked Ted. "Don't you approve of working wives?"

"I want to be able to support her," he said miserably.

"Well, my gosh," Peg said. "Some day when you're a rich practitioner I'm sure I won't be able to lift my hands because of all the heavy diamonds on my fingers, but right now it's pretty silly for me not to work, isn't it?"

"Well. . . ." Ted said cautiously.

Peg squealed, and hugged herself hard. "I'm going to get married," she said.

"That was one of the most romantic proposals I've ever heard," Ruth chuckled. "I'm happy for you, darlings."

Joe Martin and Mike Leofanti had been having breakfast at a near-by table, and they dragged their chairs over.

"We couldn't help hearing," Joe said. The old pharmacist's face was one big grin. "I insist on buying a toast to the bride-to-be." He did—five bottles of chocolate milk, and they solemnly clinked bottles before downing the milk drinks.

"I can sing 'Oh Promise Me,'" Mike Leofanti said hopefully. Peggy, remembering his rendition of *"O Sole Mio,"* at the variety show, suppressed a shudder.

"Thank you, Mike," she said politely, "but we haven't made any plans for a ceremony yet."

Joe Martin looked at Ruth. "The Jones lad seemed to be taking a turn for the better," he said. "There'll be good news coming yet, never fear."

"The kid's father is worse off than he is," Mike Leofanti said.

Ruth thought of The Wreck, his gentle smile, and his voice like blue velvet. "What do you mean?" she said.

"Well, until the boy regains consciousness long enough to talk with his father, they won't let The Wreck visit him. The poor guy is certain that his boy's a goner. I went down to his place last night. It was a pity to see him. Didn't play the piano or sing a note. Just sat there. He looked as if his world had come to an end."

Ruth thought of how his hands had caressed Seth's head the night Ed had taken her to see him.

"All on account of young Dr. Moneybags not being

able to hold his liquor," Mike said. "They ought to lock his cell and throw the key away." He finished his milk cheerfully, unaware of the chill that had fallen over the table.

"If you're talking about Dr. MacKenzie," Ruth said carefully, "you should be told that we're all friends of his."

Mike paled, then he reddened. "Uh, sure," he said. "It was only a joke, you know. He's a good guy. Well, I gotta go." He scraped his chair back and made a hurried exit.

Ted looked after him. "Worm," he said.

For a moment they sat in silence, their mood broken by Mike Leofanti's remarks.

Finally Ted sighed, and he too pushed back his chair. "Duty calls," he said. "I've got to make rounds." He looked down at Peggy. "Want to walk me as far as Revere?" he asked.

"Try and stop me," she said. "From here on in, I'm keeping close tabs on you!"

Ruth smiled as she watched them walk away hand in hand.

"That's a grand thing that's happening to them, isn't it?" Joe said.

"It really is, Joe," she agreed. "I'm happy for them."

"Your day will come, too, girl," he said. "They won't be holding the young doctor in there for long, especially now that the youngster he hit is on the road to recovery."

Ruth flushed and chose her words carefully. "I hope you're right about Allie's being released soon, Joe," she said, "but I've told you before that there's no sort of . . . understanding between us. We're very good friends, that's all."

Joe chuckled. "Sure," he said. "I know." Suddenly his face darkened. "Ruth," he said, "I've mentioned before how my friendship for your dear mother has made me feel like a father to you. Because of that, I'm going to tell you something important."

She looked at him curiously. "What is it, Joe?" she asked. "Is something troubling you?"

"Dr. Alden MacKenzie has been framed," he whispered

triumphantly. He looked around them carefully, but the near-by tables were empty, so he went on.

"That state cop fixed it so he'd face those murder charges—and do you know why?"

Ruth, shocked into silence, merely looked at him.

"Because of you, that's why. That Gillis is tough, and he's like most big-city cops: he's got no heart and he's got no conscience. He gets what he wants, no matter how. He fixed it so that—"

"Joe, stop it!" She stared at him, her eyes blazing. "Ed Gillis is nothing like that, and you know it. I know you like Allie MacKenzie very much. Well, so do I. But we have no reason to blame Ed for circumstances. He's a man who has to do his job the way he sees it. His job is an unpleasant, nasty job, but we're lucky that there are men like Ed Gillis left in the world."

He put his hand on her arm. "If I were your father, I'd forbid you to see him," he said.

"Well, you're not my father," Ruth whispered. "Can't you understand that? You're a silly old man, and you have things all confused."

He looked at her as if she had struck him, and she got to her feet and walked swiftly out of the cafeteria. For five minutes she wandered around the hospital grounds, letting her anger die. When she was calmer she felt great shame at having talked to Joe Martin the way she had, and she went back to the cafeteria to apologize. But their table was empty, and when she looked for him in the pharmacy she was told that he wasn't due to go on until that night.

Sighing unhappily, she walked to the boardinghouse. Joe wasn't there, either, so she undressed, set her alarm to ring in three hours and went back to sleep.

The bell that woke her was the telephone, not the alarm. Mrs. Hanscom was out, so she stumbled down the hall to answer the phone herself.

"Hello," she said grumpily.

"Ruth?"

It was Ed's voice, and she suddenly felt tremendously happy.

"Hello, Ed," she said.

"I just got to thinking," he said. "Tomorrow's Thursday. There's a new ice show opening in Boston. I can get two tickets."

"I love ice shows," Ruth said. Then suddenly she remembered something, and her good spirits vanished.

"Oh, Ed," she said, "I can't go."

"You can't?" Disappointment showed flat in his voice. "I'm sorry. Will you be able to see me, or is it something that will keep you busy all evening?"

"It's Allie's mother," she said. "She asked me over tomorrow night. I couldn't say no, Ed, under the circumstances. She's taking things very well, but it's a terrible ordeal."

"Sure," he said. "Do you want me to pick you up there and take you home?"

She thought of how Elizabeth MacKenzie would react to the sight of the detective who had arrested her son and sent him to jail.

"You'd better not," she said.

"Okay," he said, "if that's the way you want it."

"That isn't the way I want it," she said. But by now he was angry.

"I've got to run," he said. " 'By, now, Ruth."

"Good-by." She hung up the phone and glared at it balefully. "Run as far as you want to, you stubborn mule!"

"That isn't enough, Judge," Elizabeth MacKenzie said. "We both know that he didn't do what they say he did. I want him home with me. Call the Governor and remind him that he's going to need money to get re-elected. Break a few policemen. But don't just sit there and whine at me!" She slammed the receiver into the cradle and then sat there, trembling.

The servants had been dismissed for the evening, and the big house on Pool Hill was empty and full of echoes. *You are alone, Elizabeth MacKenzie,* they seemed to say to her. *You are all alone, all alone.*

She hoped that the telephone wouldn't ring tonight. She hoped that he would stop bothering her, let her alone. She was so tired. She needed sleep.

She started planning what she would say to him if he

108

called again: "Mr. Jones," she said aloud in the quiet room, "I'm sorry that my son's car hit your son and hurt him. It was an accident, and we all feel very badly. I shall, of course, insist on paying the hospital bills, and the insurance company will make a settlement. But you must stop calling me."

Suddenly she heard the sound of her own voice and she stopped, embarrassed. Perhaps he wouldn't even call.

Seven o'clock.

If she got through nine o'clock everything would be all right, and she could go to sleep. It was funny, but he never called after nine o'clock. She suspected it was because by then perhaps he was too drunk. He always sounded intoxicated when he called. Poor, sick, blind man.

She went to the highboy and took out her knitting. In a way, she thought, it was amusing—Elizabeth MacKenzie with her needles and yarn. She had always been too busy to take up any of the little domestic hobbies the average housewife is supposed to enjoy, but perhaps that was because she had never been an average housewife. Being the society leader of a good-sized community was a demanding job.

With Allie in trouble, though, she had wanted to do something for him herself, with her own two hands. So she was knitting him a cashmere sweater, and she found, to her surprise, that she enjoyed knitting as much as if she were one of those women, with hands chapped from dish-washing, sitting in the park gossiping all morning while they clicked their needles.

She sighed, wishing that she were, and that Allie were free to come home from the hospital to even the drabbest railroad flat.

She was nearing the end of one sleeve. She stopped knitting, trying to picture the length of his arms. She couldn't, so she gathered up her knitting and climbed the stairway to his room. The hallway was cool and dark. As soon as Allie was released, she promised herself, they would give a party, light up the house like a Christmas tree, fill it with the sound of music and laughter.

She switched on the light in Allie's room and went inside. The closet door was open and his clothing hung

109

neatly on a rack. She opened a drawer and took out one of his sweaters, a lovely tan cashmere. She spread it on the bed and covered it with the half-finished sweater she was knitting, measuring the sleeves.

Another two rows, she decided, would be enough. She folded the sweater carefully and put it back in the drawer. Her hand fluttered to the little watch which she wore pinned to the front of her dress.

Seven-twenty.

She sat in Allie's room for a while, on Allie's bed, knitting on the first thing she had ever made for him with her own hands. Finally, feeling thirsty, she gathered up her knitting and started to leave the room.

As she reached to switch off the light, the phone rang.

Let it ring, she thought. *I won't answer it. Let him ring, and maybe he'll get tired and give up.*

She reached for her knitting and started to work the needles with trembling hands.

The phone rang shrilly and insistently through the quiet old house.

Perhaps it isn't he, she thought. *Perhaps it's someone else. Suppose Alden is sick and needs me,* she thought, feeling panic settle around her with a chill.

She laid the knitting carefully on the bed.

She wouldn't say hello, she reasoned. She would merely lift the phone off the hook and put it to her ear. Then, if someone else said hello, she would talk; but if it were he she could hang up.

Go slowly, she told herself, *no need to hurry.* She walked down the stairs, toward the shrilling of the telephone in the dark hallway.

She lifted the receiver to her ear. The man on the other end of the line had started talking the moment the phone had been taken from its hook.

"My son gonna die," he blubbered. "Your son killed my boy, my little son."

She felt the strength drain out of her body. She strained to drop the receiver back into the telephone cradle.

"Your boy murderer," he wept. *"Murderer,* MUR-DERER, to do thing like that to my son. . . ."

She cleared her throat. "Mr. Jones," she said firmly,

"you're going to make yourself sick. Mr. Jones, this can't keep up, you know. Why don't you go to bed and get a good night's sleep?"

"A murderer. A murderer . . . my little boy's gonna die. . . ." He had become incoherent.

She cut him off with a trembling finger and stood there in the dark, the telephone receiver pressed into her cheek so hard that it hurt. When she lifted her finger from the phone, he was gone. After a few seconds she dialed the operator.

"I should like to register a complaint," she said.

The voice on the other end of the line was crisp and efficient, and somehow reassuring.

"What is your complaint, Madam?" it asked.

"I'm being bothered by an anonymous caller," she said, trying to keep her voice from trembling. "Is there anything you can do in a case like that?"

"Surely, Madam," the voice said; it sounded kind. "We can request the names of all callers and announce them to you before making the connection. You do not have to accept the call if you do not wish to do so. What is your name and number, please?"

She felt relieved. She gave the girl her name and telephone number, thanked her and hung up.

She walked into the kitchen. She needed something to relax her, to settle her nerves. The cook had made a Danish coffee-ring that afternoon, and she broke off a piece and nibbled it while she filled the percolator with fresh coffee and plugged it in to brew.

And the telephone rang.

She turned on the lights as she passed through the dining room and the living room. The dining-room chandelier threw a great shadow across the hall.

She picked up the receiver.

"Hello?"

It was the same operator. "I have a call for Mrs. Mac-Kenzie. The gentleman gives his name as Lester Jones. Will you accept the call?"

Why should he give his name? she thought. *Why should he give his name? As long as he's willing to give his name,*

111

perhaps I should accept the call. Perhaps he wants to apologize and end the whole thing.

"Will you accept the call?" The voice was losing its kindness, beginning to sound impatient.

"Yes," she said. "Yes, put him on."

"Ready with your call, Mr. Jones," she heard the operator say. Then there was a click, and silence.

"Hello?" she said. "Hello, Mr. Jones?"

The blubbering sounded through the earpiece once again. "Gonna have no son," he sobbed. "On accounta your boy, I'm gonna have no son. . . ."

Chapter Fifteen

On Friday afternoon, Ruth called Ed Gillis at the State Police barracks.

"I've got to see you right away," she said. "It's very important."

There was a long pause. "I'm off for the rest of the day," he said. "Can I take you to dinner afterward?"

"That will be fine," she said, "as long as you get me back to the hospital in time to get into my uniform by eleven o'clock tonight."

He picked her up in the same borrowed rattletrap. "Whose car is this, anyhow?" Ruth asked as she got in.

"Russ Johnson's," he said. "You've never met him. He's a corporal. He's married, with a small baby. He doesn't have much time for running around with the car any more, because the baby's got colic; when Russ isn't working he's either making formula for the baby or bubbling him. Funny thing, though, he seems to enjoy it." Ed chuckled.

"Very funny thing," Ruth said frigidly.

They drove along in silence.

"I'm glad you called," he said.

"I had a reason for calling," she said.

"I would have called you" he said. "I started to, maybe a dozen times, but . . ."

"What stopped you?" she asked. She half turned on the seat and stared at him. "Why didn't you?"

"There have been stories," he said. "Nasty stories. The kind of stories that could have hurt your reputation in a town like Dutton. People have been saying that I fixed it so that Allie MacKenzie would land behind bars, so that I could have a clear field with you. I thought it would be best if I stayed away, left you out of the case as much as possible."

"It never occurred to you," she said, "to ask me how I felt about the whole thing?"

"I thought I was doing the right thing," he said.

"Do you still think so?"

He slowed the car down to a crawl and looked at her. "Ruthie, I've been miserable. I've been a poor, miserable fool."

She smiled at him tenderly. "As long as you admit it, Sergeant," she said. His big hand sought her small one, and their fingers entwined.

"You'd better stop holding hands and grab the wheel," she said. "There's a law that says you have to use both hands, driving. You might be stopped by a policeman."

"I have influence," he said. "I'd see that we got adjoining cells."

They stopped for hamburgers, and Ruth told him about The Wreck.

"Mrs. MacKenzie's had all she can take," she said. "I wouldn't want her to issue a complaint against him, and she doesn't want to. For his own good, we have to convince him that his boy's going to be all right. Seth has started to talk again, and he should be out of bed and walking around in a few days."

"Why don't we take The Wreck to the hospital," Ed said. "Then we won't have to convince him. He can talk to his boy himself."

"Let's," Ruth said. "Let's go right now."

When they found him in his roadhouse, The Wreck didn't look like the man she had met on that other evening, weeks before. A stubble of unshaven beard bristled

113

from his chin, his hair was uncombed, and his tuxedo looked as if he had slept in it.

"Come on, blues man," Ed said gently, "we're going to take you to visit your boy."

He looked at them with sightless eyes. "Can I really go there?" he said. "They wouldn't let me, before." Suddenly he started, struck by a swift fear. "He's—all right, isn't he?"

"He's just fine," Ruth said. "And I ought to know. I'm his night nurse. He'll be happy to see you."

He touched her face with his fingers, tracing her features lightly.

"I remember you," he said. "Came here once before with the Sergeant. Girl with the happy laugh."

"Am I?" she asked. "I'm glad. I like the sound of that."

"Look," he said. "I can't let the boy see me like this. Give me five to clean up, huh?"

"Take ten," Ed smiled.

It was another half hour before they piled into the car, but The Wreck was a transformed man, shaven, hair slicked back and neatly parted, a pressed blue suit showing off his white shirt and blue-and-maroon rep tie.

They made the half hour drive to the hospital in silence. Sitting beside him, Ruth could feel the growing tension in the man.

"He gonna have anything wrong with him when he gets home?" The Wreck asked. "You know, anything that can't be fixed? You can tell me."

Ruth smiled gently. "No, Wreck," she said. "He's going to be as good as new."

The big blind man smiled.

Dusk was falling as they turned into the hospital driveway and parked in the parking lot. They walked slowly toward the entrance—The Wreck, between Ruth and Ed, being guided by the slight contact of his arms against theirs as they walked.

Ruth was conscious of a growing tightness in her throat.

In the elevator, she and Ed looked at one another and then looked away. Suppose Seth were asleep? It would be worth waking him up for this, she decided.

"Give me a minute to put on my uniform," she whispered as they left the elevator. "These are not visiting hours, you know, but I don't think anyone will notice us if I show you right to Seth's room. Wait here for me; I'll be right back."

Revere Ward was quiet. Far down the hall some dishes rattled faintly as collected dinner trays were lifted off steam tables and dumped into hot suds.

They paused by the door of Room 327. On the bed inside, Seth Jones was examining a tattered comic book, holding it in his thin hand listlessly, as if he had read it many times before. He was humming, a ragged, aimless tune that was a pale imitation of one of his father's improvisations. His voice was cracked and thin, the changing voice of a boy who in several years would be a man. Ruth saw The Wreck's face light up when he heard it.

"Seth?"

The boy looked up, peering into the gloom beyond the glow of his bedlamp. "Is that you, Daddy?" he said. The comic book slipped unheeded to the floor as he struggled to sit up. Ruth ran and placed the pillow more firmly behind his back.

"Your father's come to see you," she said. "Now, he can have a good long visit, but you mustn't move around like that."

"I won't," the boy promised. Guided by his son's voice, the big man moved forward until his knees touched the bed; then he knelt, his arms encircling his son.

"You going to be all right, boy?" he whispered.

"I'm all right now, Daddy," Seth said.

The Wreck's grip on the boy tightened, and he rocked back and forth wordlessly, content to hold his son in his arms.

Ruth felt like an intruder. "Come on," she whispered. Ed nodded wordlessly and followed her from the room.

In the hall he cleared his throat. "Well," he said, "the boy looks as if he's going to be all right. That's one charge Doc MacKenzie can stop worrying about."

His words brought back the problems they had been avoiding with some success all afternoon, and suddenly she felt very tired.

"Yes," she said. She looked at him levelly. "You still

115

believe Allie is the kind of man who would attack people with a knife?"

He met her glance without flinching. "Ruth," he said, "I like him. Under different circumstances I would have wanted him for my friend. But I'm a cop. I know that the man we're looking for is probably a nice, likable guy on the surface. A nice, likable guy with a sickness that's eating away at him. I also know that, ever since we took Allie MacKenzie in, there have been no more knifings."

The hospital corridor was warm and stuffy, and she felt faint, worn out by too much tension and too little rest.

"I've got a few hours yet," she said. "Let's go up to the roof and relax."

"Fine," he said softly. It was a tacit truce. Both silently agreed to let the subject lie unargued for the time being. But it stood between them as they rode the elevator up the eight floors of the hospital and stepped onto the roof.

The nurses at Memorial had a nickname for the roof: they called it "the country club." The patients had their verandas and solaria, but the roof was the property of the hospital staff. It was outfitted with shade tents and comfortable chairs, and it offered shuffleboard, quoits, and table tennis, as well as a bar which dispensed soft drinks during the daylight hours.

Now, the game area was deserted and the bar was closed. Ruth sank down onto a swing, and Ed sat beside her.

"It's peaceful up here, isn't it?" he said.

She nodded. "Yet right below us," she said, "men and women are struggling to save human lives, patients are screaming in pain, children are sobbing for their parents, and babies are being born."

He looked at her intently. "You love nursing, don't you?" he said.

"I couldn't think of another thing I'd want to do, if I had the decision to make all over again."

"That's the way I feel about police work," he said. "It's a rough job, it's a heart-breaking job—but it's a job that needs to be done."

"You do it well, Ed," she said.

"I try." He coughed nervously. "Ruth," he said, "there's a permanent opening for a plain-clothesman at the Dutton Barracks. I can have it if I want it."

Now it was her turn to stare. "Do you want it?"

"I've been told I can stay a detective, wherever I go," he said. "If I ask for it, I can get Boston duty. Which shall I take?"

Her lips felt stiff. "That's up to you, Ed," she said. "Which do you want to take?"

"Ruthie," he said, "you know where I want to be." Suddenly he was kissing her, and despite her fatigue she felt more happy than she had ever been in her life.

"Does that mean you're going to stay?" she whispered.

"That means you're going to have a very rough time getting rid of me," he said gravely. Then he grinned and looked at his watch. "Except for tonight," he said. "I've got some reports to make out." He leaned over and touched his lips to hers again. "I'll call you in the morning," he said.

"Make that in the afternoon," she corrected with a smile. "I work tonight, remember?"

His shoes made crunching noises on the pebbled roof-floor as he walked away. Ruth leaned back and closed her eyes, relaxing in the cool night air. She had almost four hours before she was due to go on duty, and she enjoyed the peace and solitude. The night was so quiet that the silence had a ringing quality, as if she were listening to the world through a big sea-shell.

Then, suddenly, he spoke to her.

"You shouldn't have let that cop kiss you like that," he said.

Ruth was startled, but she recognized the voice and made out the stooped, slender form of Joe Martin. She laughed in relief, but then she realized what he had just said, and she felt her face flush in embarrassment and anger.

"How long have you been there, Joe?"

He was leaning against a brick chimney, and he made no move to come out of its shadows.

"As long as you've been there," he said. He chuckled,

117

and somehow Ruth didn't like the sound of it. She had heard laughter like that before, but always it had come from a patient sick of mind.

"That wasn't nice, Joe," she said gently.

"Nice!" He spat the word out, and now he bounded out of the shadows indignantly. "Nice? You call kissing that cop being nice? That's no way for a daughter of mine to act."

She was beginning to feel a little frightened now, although the thought that Joe Martin could hurt anybody was ridiculous.

"Joe," she said firmly, "I'm not your daughter. I'm Ruth Mason, remember?" She got up and started toward him, thinking to take his arm and ease him toward the doorway which led to the elevator. But he sprang away from her outstretched hand like a frightened animal.

She started to follow him, but he reached into his pocket and took something out. There was a *snick* as he pressed a button in the handle of the switch-blade knife, and a shaft of gleaming steel sprang into existence in his hand.

And suddenly Ruth knew exactly who and what it was that she faced.

Chapter Sixteen

She saw their faces. Stash, Perry Watts, the fifteen-year-old boy named Leon Goldstein, the old man stabbed to death in the park. . . . Her knees buckled, but she knew that to go down was to invite attack. His usual method, she remembered, was to knife in the back. She forced herself to face him firmly.

"Joe," she said, "give me the knife."

"No," he said. "You're a bad, ungrateful daughter." Then he looked at her uncertainly. "Or are you Lee-Ann?

Lee-Ann, you shouldn't have married that West Point soldier. He'll take you away from Dutton, away from all of us."

She knew that he thought he was talking to her mother.

"Give me the knife, Joe," she said, "and I promise you that I won't go away." She held out her hand, palm up, and he smiled at her.

"If you promise, Lee-Ann," he said. For a moment she felt great relief, as it looked as though he would hand her the knife; but then she saw the crafty look in his eyes, and she pulled her palm back just as the blade slashed out at it.

"You're not fooling me," he whispered. "I see the white uniform. You're not Lee-Ann at all. You're bad, and you're going to be punished."

He stood there between her and the door, a small, bent, ridiculous-looking old man with a wild look in his eyes and a knife in his hand.

Her mind began to race.

There was little likelihood that anyone would come up to the roof at that hour. She had to discard the hope of help from someone who might happen by. And there was no other way in which she could summon aid. If she screamed, he might panic and attack her. She had no desire to die, even if it meant Joe Martin's capture.

She looked desperately over the railing of the roof, to the road which lay outside the hospital grounds. Cars moved over the road, their yellow lights sweeping past every few seconds. But she might as well have been hundreds of miles away from the motorists inside them, for all the good they could do her.

He began to move toward her.

"Joe," she said, "let's go downstairs to the coffee shop and have a cup of coffee."

She might have been talking to the stars. There was a slack smile on his face, and his eyes were dull and empty.

"Joe," she said. She noted with horror that the knuckles of the hand gripping the knife were white. He was tensed, ready to act, ready to attack. She had to retreat, and there was nowhere to go but over the side of the building. Slowly, she edged away from him, driven closer and closer to the railing.

"Joe," she said, "I won't tell anybody. We can forget about it right now. It'll be our secret, just yours and mine."

But he still kept coming.

She felt the rail against the backs of her legs, cold metal that pressed against her perspiring flesh through the thin white uniform. There was only one thing left to do, and she did it. Holding tightly to the rail, she threw one foot over onto the ledge and then the other, so that the rail was between her and her pursuer. Slowly, she began to sidle along the ledge, shuffling her feet along the cement and holding the rail with palms that were becoming slippery with perspiration.

The roof was divided into two sections, with the stairwell forming a barrier between the two. Ruth knew that once she reached the other side she could climb back onto the roof and run for aid.

But Joe was laughing. It was an enjoyable game, to him. He climbed over the rail carelessly, coming after her much faster than she could get away. She remembered how he had climbed through the tree in the woods, the afternoon he had shown her the birds' nest with the eggs in it. He had been swift and certain, like an animal.

Involuntarily, she cast a glance downward. It was an eight-story drop. She knew she could never force herself to jump.

He was almost within arm's reach when she spoke again.

"The eggs are gone, Joe."

He stopped for a moment. "What eggs?"

"The orioles' eggs," she said. "They're gone from the nest in the woods."

For a moment his eyes cleared. "They're hatched," he said. "They've flown away."

She continued to edge away. The other side of the roof was only a few feet away. She pondered the advisability of making a spurt for it. But he was so much faster than she.

"Will you take me to see the baby birds next year, Joe?" she said. She saw with dismay when she looked up at him that the sanity had died from his eyes again. He was weeping now; and he was coming toward her fast, holding the rail loosely in one hand while the other gripped the knife.

Instinctively, she stopped for a split second. Then, as the knife flashed over his head and she heard him grunt as he drove it downward, she flung herself as far to the left as she could go, without letting go her iron grip on the rail.

She felt the blade tear through the fabric of her uniform and furrow a line of fire from her shoulder to her elbow. Then, before he could raise the knife again, she struck out at him, slapping him twice in the face. She had seen sudden slaps bring hysterical patients back to reason again, and she was hoping against hope that this would happen here. But he was already off balance from the knife thrust. He teetered on the ledge for a moment like a clown on a high wire. Then, still holding the knife, he lay back on empty air as if it were a soft couch.

Ruth clung to the rail and sobbed, her eyes closed.

From far below came a scream, but it wasn't the voice of Joe Martin. Instead, it was a student nurse who had been passing near the spot where he fell.

Chapter Seventeen

Somewhere down the hall a voice called for a nurse, and she awoke with a guilty start and looked around her wildly.

"Peg," she asked thickly, "did I fall asleep on duty?" And then she heard Collins laugh, and she realized that she was in a hospital bed.

The events of the preceding night came into her memory with a rush, and she fell back against the pillow and started to cry weakly.

"There's no need for that," Peggy said softly. "It's all over now. Just try to forget about everything that's happened."

"Joe?" Ruth asked.

Peggy looked at her. "He's better off," she said. "He won't harm anyone again."

"The poor old man." She began to weep again.

"It's all over," Peggy repeated. "Put it out of your mind. Think only happy thoughts." Despite herself, Ruth had to smile weakly. She had given the same advice to patients so many times herself.

"You sound just like a nurse," she said.

There was a timid knock on the door. Ed Gillis, his hat in his hand, stood in the doorway, his face full of grave concern.

"Can I come in?" he asked.

"I was just going," Peggy said, "so you can keep an eye on her. We have orders to keep her here at least three days for observation, so don't you let her walk off."

"Three days!" Ruth exclaimed. "Not this patient. In a couple of hours I'll be ready to go on duty with the night shift."

"Not tonight, my love," said Peggy firmly. "I'll drop in later, just before I get ready to go on myself. Just think— I'll be giving *you* a back rub tomorrow morning."

The thought was a good one. Ruth settled back with a satisfied sigh. "You talked me into it," she said.

Ed looked at her for a long time; then he shook his head. "Solved my case for me, didn't you?"

"I guess I did, at that," she said.

"They tell me he cut you," he said. "Is it painful?"

She sat up in surprise. She had forgotten all about the wound. She touched her arm gingerly with her fingertips. It was bandaged. She pressed slightly, and grunted in sudden pain.

"It can't be very deep," she said. "It doesn't hurt unless I irritate it on purpose."

"Good," he said. He coughed. "I guess you know that this means Allie MacKenzie will be released."

She yelped in delight. "When?" she asked. "Will they forget about the accident, too?"

"Well," Ed said, "they won't forget about it. In all likelihood they'll fine him about a hundred dollars and take away his license for a while. But that's not too serious."

"I'm delighted," she said. "I can't wait to see him."

"I thought you'd feel that way." He heaved his bulk out of the chair and reached for his hat. "Well, I've got cases to work on that you won't be solving, so I'll be off." He touched his fingertips to his lips and then brushed her cheek with them. "Be a good girl," he said.

For a big man, she thought, it was surprising how gentle he could be.

He paused just before he went through the door.

"I got my transfer," he said. "I'm going to be stationed in Dutton."

Then he was gone before she had a chance to tell him how glad she was.

Allie MacKenzie came to see her, next morning.

"Just in time to discharge Seth Jones," he told her with a happy smile.

"How is he?" she asked.

"I went over him completely and down to the last detail, as you can imagine," he said. "Unless my years of good training have been wasted, that boy's going to live to be a hundred."

"Good for him," she said. "And now, how are you?" He didn't look too bad, she thought, considering the ordeal he had been through. The mental strain had left pouches of sleeplessness beneath his eyes, and he had lost weight, but he could rest and recuperate.

"I feel better than I have in my whole life." He reached over and took both of her hands in his own. "Ruth," he said, "I'm leaving Memorial Hospital."

She felt a sharp pang of sorrow and disappointment. "Going to buy Dr. Lohnes's practice?" she asked slowly. Then she felt ashamed of herself for feeling sorry. He

123

had been through a lot. The society practice would offer him an easy, prestige-filled life.

Allie laughed out loud. "No," he said. "I'm leaving Dutton."

"Allie!" she said. "You're not—going into research?"

He nodded, his eyes shining.

"Cancer?"

"Cancer. It's something I've always wanted to do. So little is known about the disease. Who knows? Maybe I can help to crack it."

"Allie," she said, "you're going to be good. I can feel it. You're going to be very good. Have you written to the Cancer Society yet?"

"I'm not going to take the Society fellowship," he said. "Let them give it to some doctor who needs the money."

She furrowed her brow. "I don't understand. You can't plan to outfit a laboratory of your own. You could never get the necessary facilities, the equipment, the cases. . . ."

"I'm joining the Army, Ruth," he said.

She let the news sink in for a moment. "I'm very proud of you, Allie," she said.

"It's a very specialized field, of course," he explained, "and the Medical Corps has given me a wonderful opportunity. I'm going to a research center in Nagasaki, Japan. What I learn there may be of tremendous value in the future, and it certainly won't hurt cancer sufferers now." He got up and walked to the window.

"Japan's a lovely place for a honeymoon," he said. "I'd like to book passage for two, Ruth, if you'd say the right word."

She smiled at him through tears that rushed to fill her eyes. "Allie," she said, "you tempt a girl. You really do. Logic tells me that I couldn't find a better match. And I'm so fond of you, it hurts to think that I won't be seeing you for a long while."

He sighed. "But the answer is 'No.' "

"But the answer has to be 'No,' " she said. "Don't you see?"

"Yes," he said huskily. "I do see, Ruth."

He got his coat and prepared to leave.

124

"You can do me a favor," he said.

"Anything, Allie. You know that."

"Drop in and see my mother every now and then," he said. "She's going to be lonely."

"She's not going with you?" Ruth asked.

"I wanted her to," he said, "but evidently she's been doing a lot of thinking, too. She says she'll be waiting to see me when I come home."

"She's really a very intelligent woman," Ruth said. She held out her hand and he took it. For a long moment, neither of them said a word.

"Well," he said. "I'll see you around."

"I'll see you around, Doctor," she said. He stooped awkwardly and kissed her on the cheek. Then, without looking back, he walked out of the room, down the long corridor of Revere Ward toward the elevators.

Chapter Eighteen

The invitations said that Margaret Collins was to be married to Dr. Theodore Rawlings at 10:00 A.M. on Thursday, in the chapel of Memorial Hospital. On Tuesday night, before she reported for work, Ruth sat with Ed at a quiet table in The Wreck's, and talked about the coming wedding.

"We can make it a double ceremony," he said. He reached out and took her hand. "It would be kind of rushing things, I know, but if it's all right with you . . ."

"No," she said slowly, "it isn't all right with me." For a moment a look of alarm passed over his face, and she squeezed his hand reassuringly. "Let me explain," she said, "if I can."

She sipped her coffee and chose her words carefully. "The last couple of years have been unpleasant ones for me, taken by and large," she said. "A lot of good things have happened recently. I've met some wonderful people. I've made some wonderful friends." Again she held his hand tightly. "I've met you.

"But," she continued, "a lot of terrible things have happened, too. And I've met some people who haven't been so nice. I've told you what happened in California."

"That drip couldn't have been very smart to have passed you up," Ed grinned. "I checked him off my worry list a long time ago."

She answered his grin. "Well, so have I, as a matter of fact. But the fact remains that for a while I was unhappy because of him. And then I walked straight into the nightmare business of the knifings, and what happened to Allie and Joe and Stash.

"What I'm trying to say, Ed, is that I want to spend more time doing nothing but being carefree and happy. I want to be spoiled. I want to be courted."

"You are talking to the right man," he said. "You are talking to the courtin'est man in the whole Commonwealth of Massachusetts. It will be a pleasure to spoil you." Then he paused doubtfully. "But—for how long?"

"Why don't you ask me again in six months?" she said.

"It's a date."

When they got up to leave, he nearly tripped in his haste to get around the table in time to pull her chair back for her. She smothered a giggle. "That's what I mean, darling," she said.

It was a simple, dignified ceremony, attended by a small group of their closest friends. Peg's brother Mike came to Dutton to give the bride away, and Dr. Anderson poured his wedding gift, a magnum of champagne.

Ruth caught Peggy's bouquet. "That's a pretty good sign," Ed said.

"I couldn't very well have missed it," Ruth said. She broke off a blossom and put it in Ed's lapel in place of the gardenia he had worn. "She was six inches away when she threw it."

There was a reception at a little inn in the country, and then Dr. and Mrs. Rawlings drove happily off in one of brother Mike's almost-new used cars, which he insisted they keep—at least until after the honeymoon.

Most of the women cried, and most of the men became uncomfortable, but everyone agreed it had been a nice wedding. Driving back into the city, Ruth put her head on Ed's shoulder.

"They're going to the Cape," she said.

"That's nice," he said. "The Cape's nice in the fall." He looked at her out of the corner of his eye. "If this were about six months from now, I'd say they were missing a good bet by not going camping in the mountains. Fishing, swimming . . ."

"Cleaning dirty fish, sunburn, wood-chopping . . ."

They looked at one another and laughed. She snuggled into his shoulder and felt herself slipping into half-sleep. "You know," she said drowsily, "six months is a long time."

Ed said nothing, but he grinned as he drove along the sundrenched road in silence.

There was a new girl on the ward that night to replace Peg while she was on her honeymoon. Her name was Linda Gilmartin, and she was nervous and frightened.

"This is my first job since I got my cap last spring," she said. "I've been home. My mother hasn't been well. This'll be my first taste of graduate duty. Frankly, I'm scared stiff."

"I remember," Ruth told her sympathetically. "But don't worry. That will pass."

Revere Ward was dark and silent, but the darkness and silence were old, familiar friends. Gilmartin went out on several calls, and with each call she gained confidence. In an hour she was bustling around as if she owned the hospital. Ruth grinned as she watched her.

It was after midnight when Ruth heard her call for help. She walked swiftly in the direction of the call, to find the other nurse giving an i.v. injection in room 319.

"The old man in 321," the girl said. "He's not supposed to be out of bed. But he just walked down the corridor."

"Never shout like that again," Ruth told her. "You'll alarm the patients. I'll take care of him." She hurried out.

127

She saw him leaning against the corridor wall. He was in his seventies, and he had undergone a serious operation only a week before. She knew that he must be experiencing severe nausea and dizziness.

"Mr. Pickering," she said sternly, "you are not to leave your bed again."

"I won't," he said. He looked old and hopeless, and she had to pat his arm encouragingly.

"In a day or two," she said, "you'll be able to walk around without feeling ill. Until then, you just leave the planning to us, all right?"

He smiled at her with gratitude in his eyes. "Will you help me back?"

She slipped her arm around his shoulders, and an old and claw-like hand touched her lightly on the wrist.

"Nurse," someone called from down the hall. Ruth saw with a sense of relief that the new nurse had the situation well in hand; the plea was answered before the patient could call a second time.

She walked slowly down the dark corridor of Revere Ward, feeling the old man lean upon her for support, and feeling strong in her ability to give it.